MW01164665

To Chris
A good Friend
and admired colleague

BYGONE CHRONICLE

ONCE UPON A TIME...

STANLEY J. ANTONOFF

authorHOUSE®

AuthorHouse™
1663 Liberty Drive
Bloomington, IN 47403
www.authorhouse.com
Phone: 1-800-839-8640

First published by AuthorHouse   12/13/2010

ISBN: 978-1-4520-8351-3 (hc)
ISBN: 978-1-4520-8352-0 (sc)
ISBN: 978-1-4520-8353-7 (e)

Printed in the United States of America
Library of Congress Control Number: 2010914828

This book is printed on acid-free paper.

THIS BOOK IS DEDICATED TO MY CHILDREN,
FAMILY, AND FRIENDS.
MY ENDLESS THANKS FOR ALL YOU HAVE
TAUGHT ME.

MOST IMPORTANT, I THANK MY WIFE
WHO BROUGHT ME OUT OF THE
DARKNESS AND INTO THE LIGHT.

WHEN WE MET, LIFE BEGAN.

What lies behind us
and what lies before us
are tiny matters compared
to what lies within us.

OLIVER WENDELL
HOLMES

SOMETIMES I DON'T REMEMBER
BUT I NEVER FORGET.

THE AUTHOR

SURROUNDING YOURSELF WITH DWARFS
DOES NOT MAKE YOU A GIANT.

YIDDISH PROVERB

I AM AN AFTERTHOUGHT IN MANY MINDS -
BUT NEVER MY OWN.

THE AUTHOR

Acknowledgments

In most books, those who assist and give succor to the author are acknowledged by mentioning their name and perhaps their contribution. However, because of my inadequacies with the English language, story telling, and accepting suggestions graciously, I choose not to embarrass those who have tried to assist me. Additionally, the names and specifics of my tales would touch so many still living that such a book might be actionable. Because I wish to protect the culpable, as far as it is in my power to do so, I do not use real names in the stories. Acknowledging counterfeit people serves no useful purpose. However, I thank my immediate family because, willingly or not, they are witnesses or actual perpetrators in many of the stories.

My sincerest appreciation and heartfelt gratitude to my dear friends David S., Ron G., and Walter L. for generously sharing their time reading this manuscript and putting up with my resistive nature. Because of their undeniable innocence, their real names deserve to be mentioned. Their thoughtful responses and inspired suggestions improved this book and helped its author to transcend his limitations.

How can I not acknowledge my editor extraordinaire? A wizard, his tireless assistance, compassion, and understanding of my inadequacies with language have definitely made this a better book. The accounts are mine. The proper uses of the

English language and the word smithing is his. Ron C., thank you, thank you, thank you!

To everyone else associated with this book, both the guilty and those that profess innocence, I thank you from my bottom. I believe "heart" may be missing from the previous sentence, but not from the stories.

THINGS CAN ALWAYS BE FOUND
WHERE THEY WERE LEFT

THE AUTHOR

Contents

Preface

Upon reflection, I am satisfied with my accomplishments. Many years of parenting, dentistry, teaching, and humanitarian efforts contributed to these achievements. As time passes, my short term memory becomes poorer yet my long term memory improves. Past situations constantly emerge from the corridors of my mind. I recall the funny episodes more frequently than the serious ones. However, events not memorialized in writing are often lost with the passage of time.

My childhood was filled with nightmarish exploits. Alleged sources witnessed my aggressive childhood and mischievous acts. They disclosed that I frequently fought with other kids and pushed doll carriages down stairs with children screaming. Baby sitters were not in vogue so my parents had no alternative, they had to take me along on their visits to friends and relatives. Since white shoes were stylish for small children, before a visit, my mother always applied an abundant fresh layer of polish to restore my shoe's newness. It is claimed my aggressive conduct was exhibited on these occasions. Upon encountering someone wearing dark pants, I would intentionally and repeatedly kick them, leaving white, often non removable marks on the fabric. So it is alleged by unreliable others . . . but unsubstantiated by credible witnesses and no photographs exist to validate these charges.

But memory is not faultless. Increasing age often exaggerates the actuality while memories fade or are lost. This book is an attempt to preserve history through story telling so events are not lost in the mists of time. It is a tribute to memories. I take great pleasure in recounting history and gladly share these tales. It is an intriguing idea and vanity insists I write this book. Frequently, family stories are not written down and the curious must depend on second and third hand oral narratives. Since no man lives forever and dead men rise up never, only a written chronicle can preserve the past as it fades with time.

The tales in this book are funny, some serious, all are true, except those that are contrived. But the reader is wise and will know the value of these tales. Chapters 11 through 15 should be read in sequence.

Children and grandchildren have an energetic curiosity about the biographies of their family. It is important for them to know the nature, quality, history and values of the world of their parents and ancestors. This book is written for my children who play essential roles in many of these stories. But primarily, it is written for my grandchildren who I hope will come to know and touch me through these pages.

Hopefully, other readers will enjoy the stories.

ONE

Love

Motherhood is the embodiment of love. My mother and I loved each other dearly but hers was a special love. She considered my earthly presence a wonder. In 1930, my mother gave birth to a child who only lived two days. At that time, the medical opinion was that mother would never be able to have another child. Despite the doctor's prognosis, I was born three years later and became the "miracle" birth, henceforth to be considered special and treated accordingly. I could do no wrong. This feeling permeated the entire family, much to my benefit but to the chagrin of my brother who was born five years later. Unfortunately, in mother's culture, second sons were not so special.

Mother, who was short in stature, stood a stately four feet ten inches tall. However, she was strong willed and big on determination. If my father was the head of the household, then mother was certainly his neck guiding him wherever she wanted to go. Within reason, she was able to get whatever she wanted from my father. He was a kind, softly spoken, hardworking gentlemen, who hated to refuse a request, no matter the source. Mother, on the other hand, was strong, dictatorial, irascible, and inflexible. In any confrontation, she was usually successful. Within the family there were feelings of reverence and fear of her simultaneously.

Mother was one year younger than her twin sister. That is what mother told everyone. It was not that one child was born before midnight of a new year and the other after midnight effectively giving each child a different birth year. My mother and her twin sister were both born on the same day. In fact, they were born within minutes of each other, in the same month. No matter the strength of the argument nor the person trying to convince her that this was impossible, mom would insist that there was a full year difference in their ages. Arguing with mother was impossible and a lose-lose situation. She was obstinate, intractable, and fully convinced that she was always right. Mother's philosophy was that occasionally she might not be right but she was never wrong. The discussion about birth dates persisted for a considerable time until the family decided not to bring up the subject, thus allowing mom her belief that she was one year younger than her twin sister.

One day, my Aunt told my mother that she had just received her first social security check of a few hundred dollars. Discovering she had already met the two requirements for receiving a social security check namely, working the necessary number of years and reaching the age of sixty-five, mother demanded that my father do what was necessary to secure her deserved social security check. My mom had worked hard all of her life and had reached her sixty-fifth year: she had aged one full year in thirty seconds. Fortunately, mother had graduated from public school, a special feat in 1916. It took my father several months searching through the archival records of the Board of Education in

Brooklyn to prove that, indeed, my mother was sixty-five years old. Finally, she began receiving her social security checks. Once again, peace and calm reigned in the household.

There are some who consider women the original terrorists. If this were true, my mother would be considered the Osama Ben Momma of her time. She frequently got her way because of this aggressive attitude. People did not want to be on her bad side. She terrorized our immediate and our extended family with her ideas and demands. For example, my teenage children were visiting my mom and dad in Florida. Dad intended to take the kids on a trip. Mother admonished my father not to come home if he lost the children. She meant it!

We lived in a big city. When I was ready for a bicycle, mother worried about me having an accident because she knew that I would ride the bike in the city streets with my friends. She finally allowed me to have a bicycle provided I promised to ride only on the side walk. How embarrassing? We lived in an apartment on the top floor of a four-story building and our windows faced the street. I knew she could spot me riding in the street so I had to go out of the neighborhood to ride in the gutter with my friends. Otherwise, my friends would call me a mamma's boy. When I wanted to play varsity football for my high school, she refused permission because she thought it a violent game and didn't want her "miracle" child to get hurt. It would be devastating for her. After appealing to my father for support, I received permission to play but she never went to a game. To say she was overprotective is an understatement. The difference between my mom and a Rottweiler is that a Rottweiler will eventually let go.

My mother was also paranoid. Even though we lived on the fourth floor of a walk-up apartment house, she was afraid that someone could somehow reach the roof and break into the apartment. Another concern was that entry into the apartment could be gained by using the fire escape. Because of this, the entrance door and all the windows were always double locked.

Later, after my marriage and the arrival of my children, there were occasions that mom and dad would baby sit their grand children. One of the responsibilities of the older kids was to walk the family dog. As soon as they left the house, my mother would lock the door behind them. When the dog finished his business, the children had to ring the front door bell to get back into the house.

My father, though gentle and kind, was essentially the family enforcer. He worked long hours, at times never seeing daylight on a work day. If my brother and I misbehaved, mother would "rat" on us and tell my father. She would insist on punishment. We were never frightened when my father raised his hand to punish us but became terrified and ran when he brought his hand down. My father's favorite weapon was his belt and punishment consisted of several good whacks. My brother and I discovered through experience that if we scrambled under my parents' queen-sized bed it would be impossible for my father to use the belt. Father, smarter than his sons, soon discovered that a broom handle worked well in this situation. My brother and I thought it to be the witch's broom. Guess whom we thought was the witch. Father, to us, was an overstuffed munchkin. There he was down on his knees poking under the bed with the end of the broom handle. My brother and I would move from side to side in a coordinated fashion trying to avoid the end of the broom. "He's coming on your side, no he's coming on my side." Back and forth, side to side we would move. Occasionally, father would succeed and it would smart terribly. My parents had the axiom "spare the broom and spoil the child." I always wondered about the punishment fitting the crime. Alas, I was not a legal expert.

Mother was extremely neat and meticulous. Our apartment was always immaculate. My brother and I were not allowed in the living room except if my parents had company. She would pick up our clothes wherever we left them. This became a puzzle later in my life; I could not understand why my wife would not pick up after me when I left clothes lying around our house. Mom loved hand ironing. She would iron my shirts, my undershirts, socks, and even my undershorts. My wife refused to follow this perfect example. Perhaps, she lacked that special love only a mother can give. After more than fifty years of marriage, with my wife putting up with all my shenanigans and idiosyncrasies, I am convinced she does love me because no one could be such a masochist unless they did truly love me.

Besides ironing, mom could do many things well. She could be controlling, commanding, and demanding. President John F. Kennedy once said, "Forgive your enemies but never forget them." My mother's philosophy was the same as that of actor James Cagney who declared in a movie about the Japanese in World War II, "Forgive your enemies but first get even." My mother would not forgive or forget. If you offended or disagreed with her you were put on her special list forever.

What mother could not do was cook. She was so bad she often ruined boiling water. Her religion and cooking were always in accord - everything she made was either a sacrifice or a burnt offering. Her meats were always undercooked or overcooked. Fortunately, she had a husband who always had a ravenous appetite and two sons that were close seconds to their dad. Put it on the plate and it was gone no matter the taste. My father often said that there was no such thing as bad food, just some foods taste better than others. Mom would always tell us we had to eat everything on our plates because children were starving in Europe. I could never figure out the connection between finishing what was on my plate and the starvation in Europe. Was mother going to send any left over food to the kids in Europe? Still, if she were alive today, I am certain she would admonish me to eat all my food because kids are starving in Zimbabwe. I guess she would mail the left overs to Africa.

I hated spinach. My mother insisted I eat spinach and I rebelled at the idea. I knew eventually I would lose this fight. It was the "Popeye" generation and mom felt spinach would be healthy for me. One day, I was served dinner and potatoes were on the plate. The potatoes appeared to be infested with tiny green bugs. They weren't moving and I asked what they were. "Spinach" mom replied, "I chopped them into the potatoes. You WILL eat spinach." I have to admit they were quite tasty. No one ever accused mother of being stupid.

Mother was always interested in new recipes. She never gave up trying to improve her cooking skills. After all, her abilities could only go in one direction: up. Mom's favorite recipe was for chocolate chip cookies. She often made them, taking them as gifts when she went to visit friends or relatives. The cookies, tasty because of the chocolate chips, always came out like rocks. If she could have made them uniformly round, I could have used them as skate wheels. Trying to bite into one of her cookies was like trying to bite into a ceramic floor tile. You were afraid to bite hard since you might break a tooth. Later, I discovered that dipping the cookie into a glass of milk or hot cocoa would soften them sufficiently to be chewable. I pitied my mother's friends and relatives.

Not only was my mother a great cook and baker in her own eyes, she was also an expert in interior design. My wife and I bought our first home, a beautiful, sprawling ranch house, with three levels and thirty-seven hundred square feet of living space situated on three-quarters of an acre surrounded by Oak trees. At the time, used brick was in vogue. My wife, a brilliant interior decorator, had the fire place constructed of used brick. She also designed a used brick wall for the kitchen and a used brick rack between the kitchen and family room for the storage of wine bottles. It was unusual and beautiful with the different wines showing a spectrum of colors to the visitor sitting in the family room.

When my mother first visited our home, she inspected it carefully, frequently nodding but without comments. Fortunately, she had left her white gloves home. After finishing the tour, she told us the house was beautiful. She appeared sincere but wanted to know whether we used the old, dirty bricks to save money. To her the used bricks represented a dirty, unacceptable look. However, my wife and I thought the effect was beautiful: different generations, different viewpoints. Mom felt using old, dirty bricks was not the way to save money when decorating a house. She had similar notions about the many antique fixtures we had purchased. If she knew the cost of these antique fixtures, it would have driven her crazy. I never could understand her lack of respect for something old.

There were areas in which my mother developed wonderful expertise, especially baseball. The New York Yankees and the Brooklyn Dodgers played in the 1947 World Series. My brother and I were big sports enthusiasts. Mom felt she could get closer to her sons by learning all about baseball. My brother and I began her instruction during this world series and continued until she knew all the ins and outs (no pun intended) of baseball. The following season, the New York Giants were added to the instruction list mainly because they played in the Bronx and were rivals of the Yankees and Dodgers. As her interest in baseball increased, all three radios in our apartment were tuned to the three different teams at the same time and she listened intently. She learned the names of all the players, their wives, their children, and girlfriends. Mom knew the batting averages of every player, the best pitchers, and their pitching records. This tough little lady became a walking encyclopedia of baseball.

Years later, I met a young lady and I wanted my mother to meet her. My mother was very reluctant to meet any female that I brought home. It meant the possible loss of her "miracle" child to another woman. My mother finally agreed to meet her but only at a baseball game. My future wife was not a great baseball fan and had no desire to meet my mother there. But, as usual, mom won. We all sat in the bleachers at Ebbetts Field and watched the Brooklyn Dodgers. There was little conversation, especially between my future wife and my mother. That was probably part of the plan. The wicked witch of Brooklyn had left her broom home but we all believed lightening and thunder would strike if my mom's concentration was interrupted. We all knew that my mother was so engrossed in the game that it left little time for anything else. The meeting of my mother and her future daughter-in-law was not a grand slam home run. It was more like taking a third strike.

Mom always wanted me to become a professional, specifically a doctor. Fortunately, she lived long enough to see her dream come true. I became a dentist and was the first professional in the family. Though mom believed a dentist wasn't a "real" doctor, it still gave her great pleasure presenting me as "her son the doctor." She and my father lived long enough to see me win two awards at graduation, achieve full professorship at a large dental school, operate a very successful practice, write a dental textbook, a technical book and many articles, and lecture internationally. The wicked witch of Brooklyn and her munchkin had "done good." The "miracle" produced miracles in more than one way.

TO ARGUE WITH A PERSON
WHO HAS
RENOUNCED THE USE OF REASON
IS LIKE
ADMINISTERING MEDICINE TO THE DEAD.

THOMAS PAINE

Two

Terrorism

The advent of terrorism was delineated in the Garden of Eden. How else can one explain Adam's bite out of the forbidden fruit? It must have been terror driven. Predicated on this assumption, one quickly reaches the indisputable conclusion that all women are terrorists. But why does my wife have to be the Commander-in-Chief? And why does my daughter have to be a TIT- the acronym for Terrorist in Training? All the Adams' of the world appreciate and comprehend this.

**SOMETIMES I'M NOT RIGHT
BUT I'M NEVER WRONG.**

THE AUTHOR

**THERE IS A VERY FINE LINE BETWEEN
CONFIDENCE AND CONCEIT.**

THE AUTHOR

THREE

Theory of relative-ity

Though many believe marriages are created in heaven, there is no such thing as perfect connubial bliss. Friction and dissidence occur in every relationship. Even though they may be a loving, caring, and devoted couple, oftentimes, without malice aforethought, one partner makes a comment or does something disagreeable to the other, creating dissension and manufacturing tension.

Because of the conflicts and differences of opinion in most marriages, perhaps abetted by a lack of a direct DNA connection, my wife postulated her THEORY OF RELATIVE - ITY.

If we compare Einstein's Theory of Relativity to my wife's Theory of Relative-ity, we note an obvious difference in their equations. Similarities, however, occur in their universality and difficulty of comprehension. Unquestionably, each formula drives its particular universe.

EINSTEIN SPOUSE

$$E = MC^2 \quad I = WE^2$$

I leave the reader to explore the meaning of Einstein's Theory of Relativity. The scientific explanation of my wife's Theory of Relative-ity follows.

Marriage vows stipulate that husband and wife shall love and obey each other until their death, and perhaps beyond. There are antagonists to these conditions who argue that marriage is death incarnate. In my wife's Theory of Relative - ity, the "I" in the equation stands for husband or wife individually and promotes equality, while the WE^2 stands for the couple collectively, as one unit, inseparable. By definition, a statement or promise made by either partner causes the liability to reside with both. My wife's interpretation of this new scientific formula suggests that I will be bound by any commitment she makes.

Additionally, based on the originality and authority of my wife's accurately deductive, methodically sound, scientifically proposed Theory of Relative-ity, if she is "I" and I am one-half of the combined WE^2, than she is a little more equal than me because I am the smaller half of the collective WE^2.

Four

The blackout

Shortly after five p.m. on November 9, 1965 I was treating a patient in my dental office when suddenly the lights flickered for a few seconds and then went back on full bright. Everyone paused for the moment and then returned to their tasks. Moments later the lights blinked again, more slowly and for a longer period. They went back on. Within minutes, the flickering recurred. This time the lights went out completely and everyone was startled, but there was only silence surrounded by darkness. Everything came to a standstill. I felt blind and I wondered if blind people can see in their dreams. It was New York City, and the beginning of the Great Blackout.

Other than the flickering, there was no warning the lights would go out permanently. We were totally unprepared for what followed. The patient being treated was the mother of one of my dental students. I taught at the dental college and students frequently referred their family and friends to me. When the darkness came, it created a very spooky and fearful atmosphere. Some say real men are never afraid of the dark. For the first time, I questioned my manliness.

At first, we thought the lack of light would last for a short period, so we joked about many things. Wasn't it amazingly coincidental that all the light bulbs burned out at the same time? Where could we buy replacement light bulbs quickly? Was this, by design, an event caused by the angel of darkness? What if the blackout lasts for a long time? Will it get cold? What will we do? Beyond all these questions we realized the immediacy of the problem, our inability to work because all dental equipment runs on electricity.

A call to the building's maintenance department revealed they too were in the dark about the prospects of the lights coming back on. Suddenly, someone remembered they had a pocket transistor radio. After learning that the blackout had affected most of the Northeast, it became apparent we would be without electricity for a long period. We began searching for any form of illumination. At this point, a large jar of lightening bugs would have been helpful. We tried using matches and cigarette lighters but these proved ineffective. Ultimately, I sent my assistants scurrying to offices throughout the building seeking candles or flashlights to borrow, buy, or steal. We did have natural gas, so we used a Bunsen burner for some visibility. This, too, proved ineffective.

Shortly, one of my assistants returned with a flashlight, compliments of a neighbor in an adjacent office. It became a perplexing comedy, one flashlight and three people needing it. The most urgent task was the replacement of temporary crowns for my patient. One assistant held the flashlight and directed the beam at the patient's mouth while I worked. If a particular material was not at hand, I had to stop while the flashlight was passed from one assistant to another in order to secure the item I needed. It was "Tinkers to Evers to Chance," the famous baseball double play combination, and if anyone dropped the "ball" the rest of us were plunged back into darkness. Without light from the flashlight, the slightest turn and one of us would bump into something or knock some object over. Somehow we muddled through.

I suddenly realized that if the entire city was dark because of a lack of electricity, neither the elevators nor the trains would be running. My assistants lived in the city and would be able to walk home. It would be a long trek but they were young. Additionally, they were all wearing flat, comfortable, working shoes conducive to walking. On the other hand, my patient, in her early fifties, was wearing high heeled shoes which would make it impossible for her to walk to Brooklyn.

I lived on Long Island and usually took a train to work. It ran on electricity, but not tonight. Fortunately, I had my car in the city. It occurred to me that I could drive my patient home. It was out of my way, but it was the noble thing to do. I realized that after dropping her off, I could visit my mother-in law. She was a warm and welcoming person who lived not far from my patient. Two birds with one trip! Furthermore, my mother-in-law, a wonderful cook, had a gas stove. I was certain of a delicious meal. The plan was falling into place: descend to the street level; retrieve the car; drive my patient home; go to my mother-in-law for dinner, and then home to my wife and kids on Long Island.

At that moment, the telephone rang. Perhaps it was a patient canceling an appointment for the next day? Not likely. My secretary answered the phone and said it was my wife. I picked up the phone and my wife explained that due to the blackout there was no electricity, no heat, the house was freezing, and she did not know what to do to keep herself and the kids warm. We had only moved into our new home in Farmingdale, Long Island about six weeks ago, and many things were still unfamiliar to her.

I suggested she collect lots of blankets and pillows, place

them in front of the fire place, gather the children and lay down all together as though camping out. Then light a fire. "I don't know how to light a fire," she screamed, exasperated. "Relax honey! Just relax!" I pleaded. "I can't help you from here but only give you advice. Getting upset will not help the situation." I paused for a second, "there are plenty of logs adjacent to the fireplace. First, put some newspaper on the grate, then place some kindling on top of the paper. You'll find kindling near the logs." I spoke to her as I would to a child, trying to simplify everything so she would understand and not become upset. "Now, strike a match and light the paper. When the kindling begins to burn, place a small log on top. When this log begins to burn keep adding additional logs until you get a roaring fire. Don't put too many logs on all at once or you will smother the fire. The fire and the blankets will keep you warm. And for goodness sake" I shouted, "make sure the flue is open."

"What the heck is that? Where do I find that?" my wife shot back panicking, probably caused by all the instructions.

"An open flue allows air to travel up the chimney. You'll find the lever inside the fireplace, on the left side," I continued. "Push it forward and it will open the flue. *Make sure you do it before you start the fire,*" I emphasized. "In fact, let your oldest son do it. He's ten years old and supposedly a big shot Cub Scout. Give him the job. The flue must be open or the room will fill with smoke after you light the fire. When the flue opens you will hear a 'click.' Before lighting the fire have your number one son look up the chimney. He should be able to tell whether the flue is open." Pausing for a second, I entreated, "Do you understand?"

"I . . . think . . . so," she responded, with a distinct quiver in her voice.

"I 'think so' is not good enough," I commented. "If you don't do it right, you're going to have big problems. Do you want me to repeat everything?"

"No! I got it all!" She paused, then continued, "What do you intend to do?"

"We are about ready to leave. I'm going to drive my patient to her home in Brooklyn and then proceed to your mother for something to eat. Think she'll cook for me?" I paused for a second. "She better, otherwise, I'll give you back to her. After eating, I'll come straight home. Don't worry about me. As Yogi Berra says, 'I'll be there when I get there'."

With that, I hung up the phone. In my heart I was certain she understood what had to be done. I knew that everything would work out. She was a very capable person but she sometimes became overwhelmed with anxiety. In retrospect, it worked out exactly as planned.

The descent

We were ready for our voyage into darkness. We agreed to descend the stairs in a group and to stay together no matter what happened. Common sense dictated that the flashlight should be held by someone in the back of the group so everything forward would be illuminated. One of my assistants had this responsibility. I decided to lead the group for if someone tripped there was the possibility of my stopping their fall. Who held the flashlight and who would be the group leader was not discussed because there were three women in the group and I did not want to provoke an argument. I knew there were theories relating to arguing with a woman and was absolutely certain none worked.

We made certain the Bunsen burner was extinguished, turned off all the light switches and locked the office door. The stairwell door was around the corner from the office and we slowly proceeded there. The flashlight was not very powerful and the illumination in front was meager. The light coming from the rear caused shadows to dance along the walls, creating a very eerie feeling.

Soon, we were at the stairwell door. I expected light from the emergency system, but when I opened the door the stairwell was pitch black. Obviously, the backup emergency lighting system was not working. I set a slow pace so everyone could follow in single file and still hold on tightly to the bannister. In this fashion, with the light pointed downward and coming from the rear, there was adequate illumination. Down we went, one followed by another. Some say going down a flight of stairs is easy, but inadequate lighting makes it treacherous. Making the descent even more difficult was the type of stair; concrete, with a steel top and edge. The steel is placed on the step to prevent concrete breakage. But the steel feels slippery when stepping on it, and in the dark, it made the descent more troublesome.

The building had sixty floors, but fortunately we only had fifteen flights of stairs to descend. We did not see anyone from our floor and did not hear any sounds on the floors below. It took us longer to leave because we had to complete the patient's treatment and perhaps they had left earlier. Because we moved so slowly, our progress felt like we were stuck on a stopped escalator. It was so quiet I could hear the distinct sounds of our footsteps on the stairs. Our heavy breathing was also audible. At each landing, we momentarily paused to make sure that everyone was okay. We then resumed our descent. Whenever we stopped, someone always had a funny comment to make to relieve the tension. It was wonderful because it helped reduce stress and anxiety and made time pass more quickly.

"Hey! This is like exercising," was one comment. "Does that mean we will die healthier?" A rather morbid thought.

Stopped on another landing, someone shouted, "Hey, it sure is dark in here. It reminds me of the Invisible Man marrying the Invisible Woman. Ya' know their kids weren't much to look at." The laughter was calming.

A little later, I asked if anyone heard the classical dental joke? Not receiving an answer, I continued. Well, a woman goes to the dentist and complains of a toothache. After an examination and x-rays, the dentist tells the woman her tooth has to be extracted. The woman responds, "Oh my goodness, I'd rather have a baby." The dentist replies, "Well make up your mind lady so I'll know how to adjust the chair."

"Hey, Doc!" someone called out from the landing above. These were tenants from the floors above us who, because of our delay in leaving, had caught up with us. They had joined our group and were using our light source to help their descent. I looked up, and in the dim light recognized the face of one of my patients. "Listen to this one," he continued. "An 86-year-old-man walks into a crowded physician's waiting room. As he approaches the desk, the receptionist says, 'yes sir, what are you seeing the doctor for today?' "

"There's something wrong with my penis," he replies in a loud voice.

The receptionist becomes irritated and says, "You shouldn't come into a crowded doctor's waiting room and say things like that."

"Why not? You asked me what was wrong and I told you."

The receptionist replies, "You obviously caused some embarrassment in this room full of people. You should have said there is something wrong with your ear or some other part of your anatomy and then discussed the problem further with the doctor in private."

"You shouldn't ask questions in a room full of people if the answer could embarrass anyone. I'm out of here!" says the man and he walks out of the room.

Several minutes later he re-enters the room.

The receptionist smiles smugly and asks, "Yes?"

"There's something wrong with my ear," he states.

The receptionist nods approvingly and smiles, knowing he has taken her advice. "And what is wrong with your ear, Sir?"

"I can't pee out of it," the man replies. The entire stairwell became enveloped in laughter.

"Hey," came another loud voice from an invisible man on

the landing above. "We don't have any electricity, but I know a guy who always can tell in which direction an elevator is going to go. He stands outside the elevator door and when you ask him if he knows whether the elevator is going up or down, he responds, 'That's right.' "

Again laughter and chuckles. As we continued down the stairway, our group was joined by others. As we got closer to the street level, our flashlight became dimmer; the batteries were beginning to fail. It became more difficult for me to see. Walking down the last few flights, I operated mostly by Braille, never letting go of the bannister and using the heel of my shoe to determine the exact location of the steel tip of the step. It was slow and tedious, but effective.

At every landing, I would announce the floor number so everyone would know the number of flights remaining. On the eighth landing, one of my assistants had to go to the bathroom. Taking our only flashlight, she was accompanied by another of my assistants. When they left, the procession stopped and we returned to darkness. While we were waiting, someone remarked about a woman who lost a one hundred-yard breast stroke race because the other racers were unfairly using their hands. We all agreed the complaining woman had to be a blonde. This prompted someone to inform us that blind people do not like to sky dive because it scares the dog. The joke telling, good or bad, brought us closer.

When the women returned with the flashlight, we continued our journey. It took more than one hour to descend the fifteen flights. When we opened the door to the lobby, it appeared as though the lights had come back on. After being in the dark for so long, the light temporarily blinded us. The building's security personnel had set up emergency lights and they were welcome. At this point, the building was mostly empty other than us, the few people following us, and the security guards. We had proved the Law of Location: No matter where you go, there you are.

We went into the street and were amazed. The usual cacophony of city sounds was absent, no car horns or the groveling sounds of a large crowd. Occasionally, the piercing sound of an ambulance's siren or a police car was heard in the distance.

We all kissed and hugged and said our goodbyes. We wished each other well and my assistants left to go to their homes. My patient and I walked to the garage where my car was parked; it was a block and one-half away.

While walking, we heard chatter and gaiety among the pedestrians as they wended their way through the city to accommodations at a hotel or a friend's home. It could have been a time of fear, disorder and panic, but there was none evident. Without any functioning traffic lights, street traffic was chaotic. However, at every intersection citizens, acting as volunteer cops, attempted to control traffic. Though the evening was cool, several of these men had removed their jackets so their light-colored shirts were more visible. What helped immeasurably was the light emanating from a brilliant full moon. We noted restaurants full of Diners and bars three deep with stressed commuters. In the face of adversity, people bonded together. The blackout had affected people and they came together with a level of friendliness and support that was usually rare in the City. Everyone joined together to eat, drink and to share their mutual concerns. New Yorkers, usually estranged from one another, now became neighbors and friends and their noble actions became evident.

We arrived at the garage and I gave the attendant my parking stub. Without electricity to run the time stamp machine, there was no charge for parking. When the attendant returned with my car, I gave him a suitable tip, my patient climbed in, and we were ready for the next stage of our journey.

The journey

Exiting the garage on East 40th Street, I proceeded cross town to Second Avenue. The evening was not cold so we were able to drive with the windows partially open. The usual sounds of the street were no longer evident. Instead, chatter and merriment dominated. People sat on chairs and on their stoops outside their homes; others stood around. Some waved at the car as we passed. Our bright headlights momentarily lit up the darkness.

We slowed, made a right turn onto Second Avenue and a left turn onto 34th Street. This took us to the Franklin D. Roosevelt Drive (East Side Drive) where a right turn led us South toward Battery Park.

The trip on the East Side Drive was remarkable. In the brilliant moonlight, the skyline of the buildings in Queens was clearly visible. There were hardly any other cars. I used my bright lights for maximum illumination. It reminded me of driving on narrow country roads in England with only the car's headlights lighting the roadway. Additionally, the high beams momentarily lit up the walkways and jogging paths found along the Drive. Around every bench or walkway people, who probably never met before, were sitting, standing, and conversing. Amazingly, despite the dark, there were joggers. As they ran, the bouncing light created by the flashlights they held produced silhouettes resulting in eerie effects. One jogger had mounted a flashlight on top of his head, like the light in a miner's hat, further evidence of man's ingenuity in an emergency. Moonbeams reflected off the East River interrupted only by the passing of a tug boat, its cabin illuminated by electricity from the boat's generators. Different colored running lights, white, red, and green, mounted atop its high wheelhouse made the boat look like a Christmas tree gliding across the water.

As we continued, we could see the faint outline of the

Manhattan and Brooklyn Bridges against the moonlit sky. Pedestrians walking across the bridges on their way to Brooklyn appeared like little moving specks. In spite of the adversity, people were going home.

Shortly, the East River Drive became South Street, which became the West Side Highway. We took the Battery Tunnel exit, went through the tunnel, did not have to pay a toll because of the lack of electricity, and continued to the Prospect Expressway, which became Ocean Parkway. While driving in Brooklyn, once again we marveled at the people sitting on benches or standing around.

We arrived at Avenue N and I made a right turn. My patient lived in the corner apartment house. She thanked me profusely for taking her home and promised that for the remainder of her life she would never be without a flashlight in her purse. A group of her neighbors came over to greet her.

"Where have you been? Are you O.K.?" one of them asked. "You'll never believe my story," she began. "I was trapped on the fifteenth floor in my dentist's office . . ."

It was about nine p.m. when I arrived at my in-law's home and I was starving. After receiving hugs and kisses from both, I noticed a look of grave concern on their faces. "What's the matter?" I asked. "You both look very upset."

"We are sick with worry," my mother-in-law replied. "We haven't heard from Lewis. We have no idea where he is."

Lewis was my wife's older brother. He had an accident at birth which resulted in spastic, cerebral palsy. This caused him to walk with a disturbed gate and affected his speech; however, he was smart and extremely strong. At times, Lewis would grasp my wrist and I wouldn't be able to break his grip. When he was born, specialists knew little about treating educationally and mentally retarded people so, for all practical purposes, he never learned to read or write. For most of his adult life, he held a messenger's job. It did not make a difference whether it was pouring rain or snowing, Lewis was relentless and would push on until the delivery was made. He worked for many years in the vicinity of the Empire State Building and the traffic cops knew him. When he was on a route to one of his customers and approached the intersection at Fifth Avenue and 34th Street, one of the busiest intersections in New York City, the patrolman on the corner would stop the traffic so he could proceed uninterrupted. Lewis often ignored the "do not cross" sign and assumed the vehicle's driver would see him and stop. Fortunately, it always worked.

Lewis was an idiot savant of travel. He knew the numbers and routes of every bus and train. He could direct the most naive traveler to any part of the New York metropolitan area. As a child, Lewis once became lost in Manhattan and was eventually found by a policeman. Lewis got into the patrol car and without knowing his address, he was able to direct the policeman to his home in Brooklyn. He was eight years old at the time. In my heart, I was certain Lewis was O.K.

"Don't worry, Mom." I responded. "Lewis is no dummy. I'm sure he's O.K." As I was completing the sentence, Lewis walked into the room.

"Where have you been?" my mother-in-law screamed. "Dad and I have been worried sick. Don't you care how we feel? Couldn't you have called us to say you're O.K.?"

"I'm sorry," replied Lewis. "I'm sorry," he repeated. Lewis was forty years old at the time.

"Well, where have you been?" shouted my mother-in-law again.

"What do you mean, . . . what do you mean, 'where have I been?' " answered Lewis in an agitated tone. He continued, "I've been on the streets walking home. That's where I've been."

"You mean you walked all the way from Manhattan?" interrupted my father-in-law.

"That's right," he replied. "There's no electricity so there are no trains running, remember?"

Lewis had walked from his job in Manhattan, over the

Manhattan Bridge, into Brooklyn and then home. It was after nine p.m., which meant he had been walking more than four hours. The distance he walked was about eight miles, an amazing effort and a tribute to his strength, directional abilities, and perseverence.

Everyone relaxed. I requested something to eat for Lewis and me. I knew Lewis did not stop to eat; he would not until he got home. I was starving. To reinforce my demand, I threatened my mother-in-law that I would return her daughter to her but would keep the grand kids if she didn't feed me.

"Over my dead body," she exclaimed. "I have some left over brisket and fresh rye bread. How does that sound?"

"If that's the best you can do I'll have to settle." I pumped my fist and shouted under my breath, "Yes."

After finishing a great brisket sandwich with iced tea, I paid my respects to everyone and departed for home. It was now past ten p.m. consequently I refrained from calling home out of fear I would wake up my wife and the children. I assumed they were sleeping peacefully in front of the fireplace.

Home

I jumped into my car and began my exodus from Brooklyn. In a short while I was on Long Island finishing the last leg of this exhaustive adventure. Long Islanders believe you should never leave a safe distance between you and the car in front of you, or the space will be filled by another car. As the other car fills the space, you slow down to again create a safe distance and another car pulls in front of you. It almost feels as if you are going backwards. Tonight, this was no problem because no other cars were on the road. Without traffic, I was able to stay in the middle lane and speed doing at least sixty miles an hour. I expected to be home in twenty minutes.

Suddenly, it occurred to me that in the confusion of the day, I had not recently checked the gas gauge. I knew it was full when I started out in the morning, but when I looked at the gauge the needle was pointing at empty. Gas stations would be closed because pumps need electricity for power. I remembered something my father told me while he was teaching me to drive. "Son," he said, "as long as the gauge's needle moves, there is some gas in the tank." He continued, "when the needle mechanism sits on the bottom of the gas tank, the needle cannot move indicating the engine is basically running on fumes." The needle was moving! Thank goodness. But how much gas is left? How long will it take for the remaining gas to be consumed? Two minutes? Ten minutes? There was no way to know. I slowed the car to forty miles per hour because at slower speeds gas consumption is more efficient producing more miles to the gallon.

Anxiety caused me to look at the gas gauge repeatedly. I glanced at the road, then quickly glanced back at the needle. Up and down went my head, again and again. I was frustrated and unnerved waiting for the needle to stop wiggling. I was resigned that if the car ran out of gas, I would roll it onto the shoulder using its remaining momentum, lock it up, and walk the rest of the way home. I guessed that I was about five to ten miles from my home.

The needle kept moving. Way to go baby! I was listening to the car radio throughout the drive home and the refrain from "Somewhere Over the Rainbow" hung in the air. Perhaps this would prognosticate something good. I looked up and suddenly, in the distance, there appeared to be murky rays of light filtering through the trees. I was traveling East and it was not a rainbow nor the sun rising. I quickly looked down and the needle was still oscillating. Looking up again, the light seemed brighter. Down I looked, and the needle now seemed to have stopped moving; I was unsure. I came to a curve in the road and it was dangerous to look down. As I rounded the curve, the light appeared even brighter. The blackness and the light were commingled, taking on a misty, hazy appearance. The road straightened and now the entire sky was lit like a giant fireball. But there was no yellow color in this light. It was like a mushroom cloud, but stark white, enhanced by the black backdrop. There was no other light except this cloud like apparition. I quickly looked down, the needle had stopped moving. Oh well! I took my foot off the gas and allowed the car to roll on its own momentum. I figured to go as far as it could. The light was getting brighter. Brighter and brighter still, and then the car began to sputter, but continued rolling forward. At this point, the light was so bright it blinded me momentarily. When my eyes became acclimated to the intense light, I realized it was emanating from a gas station. Like a miniature baseball field, the station was all lit up by a ring of floodlights surrounding its center. Hence, its appearance as a cloud like apparition or a space craft.

A gas station with blazing floodlights had to have electricity. I guided the sputtering car to the nearest pump. An attendant came out and inquired how he could help me. I replied with gusto, "Fill her up, please."

I learned from the attendant that the station had its own generator. I was his first customer in the past three hours and he was glad to see me. I could not describe how happy I was to see him. With the gas tank full, I started home. The trip was short, the anticipation immense, and soon I was on my driveway. I decided not to put the car in the garage because the noise created by opening the door might awaken everyone. I parked on the driveway, exited the car, and walked to the front entrance. I opened the door, and to my surprise and delight my children jumped all over me. Hugs and kisses were exchanged by all. I spotted my wife standing in front of the roaring fire. We made eye contact and she slowly walked toward me. The children made space and I put my arms around her and pulled her tightly toward me. Initially she was tense, but her body soon began to sag as the stresses dissipated. The family was together, safe and sound. We walked to the fire place and cuddled in front of the fire. Shortly, sunrise dispatched the darkness.

Lewis died in a nursing home at age seventy-nine. He always knew where everything was and always directed visitors appropriately.

Each time my patient returned to my office for treatment, she showed me the flashlight she carried in her pocketbook. I completed her dentistry about six weeks after the blackout, and the next time we met was two and one-half years later at her son's afternoon dental school graduation. She immediately put her hand into her pocketbook and pulled out a small, fully functional flashlight. She was prepared for the next blackout.

THERE COMES A TIME IN A MAN'S LIFE . . .
AND I'VE HAD MANY OF THEM.

CASEY STENGEL

YOU CANNOT LOSE SOMETHING
YOU NEVER HAD.

ANONYMOUS

FRIENDSHIP IS THE STUFF
THAT NOURISHES LIFE.
THE AUTHOR

FIVE

Sticks and stones

Sticks and stones may break my bones but names will never harm me - except when they need to be remembered. When I cannot recall someone's name, I am embarrassed. Socially, it is a disadvantage, since the inability to remember names exerts an influence on friendships thus impeding the socialization process. The only name I remember consistently is my own, because I deal with myself constantly.

I did not say I forget; I never forget. I just do not always remember. Recalling information has been a lifelong problem. I have great difficulty retrieving names or facts when they are needed. I often retrieve them ten minutes, two days, or even a month later. Something stimulates my memory; the information pops into my head. There are times when recalling the information will wake me in the middle of the night.

Recall involves retrieval of information from long term

memory without hints or cues, whereas recognition involves object identification using hints or cues to which you have been previously exposed. I am wonderful at recognition but terrible at recall. Presented with a picture of a person or place accompanied by a list of names, I will make the correct association easily.

Recalling a cousin's or friend's name puts me in a delicate situation. My wife, who understands my problem, is frequently a great help. Before going to a party or function, she names the people we will most likely meet. When we unexpectedly meet someone we know, she always mentions that person's name thus avoiding an awkward moment for me.

I remember once calling out to one of my sons,

"Hey Sammy, can you come over here for a moment please?"

With that request, my son crossed the room, approached me and responded,

"Dad, I love you very much but I'm thirty-four years old and it's about time you remembered my name is Ben."

YESTERDAY IS BUT TODAY'S MEMORY, AND TOMORROW IS TODAY'S DREAM.

KAHIL GIBRAN

Six

I c u

Youngpeople often have a strong sense of immortality and believe they are immune to harm. These "immortals" feel youth entitles them to long, vigorous, productive lives, so they do not take potential life threatening incidences seriously. Because they feel invincible, the young do not deliberate over death. At best, they have a grudging acceptance of their own mortality. They function without considering possible dire consequences, counting on some unknown entity to carry them through adversity.

Good fortune always seems to follow me, though I have had my share of reverses. Yet, at critical times, a catalyst appears, such as a supportive person or an event, which turns the tide.

It began after supper on a Friday night. Before eating, I had changed from my business attire to beat-up, old clothing. When the meal was over, I sat down in my favorite chair to watch a televised basketball game. Several minutes passed, and suddenly I felt a burning sensation in my chest. It was a heavy meal, and as usual I had eaten excessively. I had no special thoughts about this sensation other than it was causally related to my overeating. I was no stranger to heartburn.

About 11:00 p.m., I went to bed after the basketball game ended and tossed and turned most of the night. Even though this uncomfortable feeling was the etiology of a very unfavorable night's sleep, I was convinced the burning sensation was heartburn. When I awoke the next morning, the awareness was milder, but still noticeable.

My friend Jerry and I went to a health club every Saturday morning. It was a new, co-ed club, and we were among its first members. It was tastefully decorated, carpeted throughout, and soft music played without interrupting commercials. There were tread mills, workout stations, and a large sauna which held several members at one time. Jerry and I were usually tense, a reaction related to on-the-job pressures that occurred during the previous week. Vegetating in the sauna for an hour followed by a massage and nap helped us relax our bodies and minds. I always treated indigestion as a passing nuisance. Long live the immortal.

After one hour in the sauna, the burning feeling became more intense. Our conversation was so animated, as was usually the case, complete with jokes and stories of the preceding week, that it was easy to disregard the increasing intensity of my chest discomfort. Laughter is truly a wonderful cure.

Completing my stay in the sauna, I submitted my body to a glorious, relaxing one hour massage. As the masseur moved his magical hands over the various parts of my body, I would slip in and out of a somnolent state. The burning awareness all but disappeared.

One hour in the relaxation room was next. When I awoke from my nap, I felt fantastic. The burning sensation was almost gone. I showered, dressed, said goodbye to "Jer.," and proceeded home to lunch with my wife.

The day was beautiful. It was early December, cold, a blue sky with thick billowing clouds, fortunately no wind and no sign of snow. The trees were barren, the colorful leaves having fallen long ago, and a winter feeling was in the air. While driving home, I heard a "bam," and then felt a thump, thump, thump from the rear of the car. I pulled over to the side of the road, exited the car, and much to my chagrin discovered a flat tire. What a bummer. As I changed the tire, the indigestion returned and became more intense. This did not concern me because, other than the discomfort, I was really feeling good. Immortality!

After arriving home, I lunched with my wife, and spent the rest of the day relaxing. Sleep that night was uneventful, and when I awoke the next morning the burning sensation was barely noticeable. If I had any thoughts of a heart attack, they were undermined by a sense of immortality. I recently celebrated my fortieth birthday; had many grandiose plans, and there were many things yet for me to accomplish. Ah, immortality.

Sunday mornings were regularly reserved for tennis. I was always athletically active and enjoyed running around, assuaging my anger and frustrations by hitting a small, unprotected ball. Working up a good sweat was tantamount to a religious rite, so I looked forward to these doubles matches.

In the summer, we played outdoors but in the winter our matches were held in a tennis bubble containing six Hard-True courts. The courts were reserved for two hours and I was one of four regular players. I was never an outstanding tennis player, but who cared? For two hours, I worked up a good sweat, was relaxed, and that was all that mattered.

We began playing at 9:00 a.m., and as the matches progressed the intensity of my indigestion markedly increased. There never was any pain. I began sweating, more profusely than usual for these matches, and became more and more sluggish. Losing my usual quickness, it felt as though I was playing in slow motion. At one point my opponent hit a lob over my head. Under normal circumstances I might have spun around, tracked down the ball and returned it. But my legs were so weak I knew I would not have a chance to retrieve the ball so I hollered "yours," and smiled at my partner. There was no way my partner could have retrieved that lob.

As I drove home after the tennis match, I began to entertain the notion that maybe my diagnosis was incorrect and perhaps indigestion was not the cause of my feeling poorly. If this were true, would going to work the next day be smart? It would be Monday, a school day. I had a teaching position at the dental school and if I did not appear students counting on me for help would be disappointed. Ah, the power of one's ego. I would make the decision later in the day, I thought, depending upon how I felt. Pure procrastination.

Finally, I made the dreaded determination to stay home and not go to school. My wife insisted I take something for the indigestion, and, to avoid her nagging, I acquiesced to her demand. I slept most of the day and by the evening I felt wonderful. Rested and reinvigorated, the burning sensation in my chest was hardly noticeable. The medication had worked, or so I thought. On hindsight, it was the rest that worked not the medication. Had I gone on vacation for a couple of weeks the indigestion probably would have disappeared completely.

The following morning, I started out for work well rested with the burning feeling in my chest hardly noticeable. While walking up the long flight of stairs, however, the intensity of the burning sensation in my chest began to increase and my breathing became labored. But, when I rested at each landing the intensity decreased. I just was not reacting to these obvious signals.

As I walked to my office, the burning sensation became increasingly intense accompanied by a greater difficulty breathing. I could hardly catch my breath. Repeated stops were made, and with each rest period I felt a little better. Yet, when I started walking again, my breathing difficulties became exacerbated even though I walked increasingly shorter distances between rest periods. A concerted effort over an inordinate amount of time finally brought me to my office.

It was time for me to call my internist, who was also a cardiologist. I got "Heshey" on the phone, explained my symptoms to him and he thought I was having a heart attack. He recommended I immediately go to the nearest hospital or, at the very least, come to his office for an Electrocardiogram (EKG).

I did not want to go to the nearest hospital, a dumb decision, so I called my friend "Jer." who picked me up and delivered me to "Heshey's" office.

This is where the story becomes bizarre. His nurse quickly brought me into "Heshey's" inner office and an EKG was taken. The diagnosis - I was having a heart attack.

"Heshey" told us he was going to call the hospital and request a bed for a patient having a heart attack. He told us the admission's operator would inform him that the hospital is full and there are no available beds. As soon as a bed becomes available, she will call Dr. "Heshey." It is the most ridiculous thing I ever heard. The patient might die yet the hospital did not want to be inconvenienced.

"Heshey" was on the staff of the hospital and anticipated their response. He told "Jer." to drive me to the hospital as quickly as possible and go directly to the emergency room. He is to tell the emergency room staff that he suspects I am having a heart attack. Under these circumstances, they cannot turn me away because of fear of a legal suit should I die. "Heshey" said the hospital will find a place for me somewhere and he will come to see me as soon as I am admitted.

"Jer." followed "Heshey's" instructions. He took me to the hospital emergency room, they gave me several tests, they took blood, and then gave me another EKG. Their verdict - I was having a minor heart attack. For me, the word minor was a hindsight word. I wondered whether this is like being slightly pregnant. The doctors told me my heart attack did not appear to be serious. I wondered, aren't all heart attacks serious? For the first time in my life, I was scared and was not feeling immortal.

The attending doctors told me they were going to order an intravenous (IV) set-up and give me a sedative, standard treatment for heart attack victims. While the nurses were preparing for these procedures, I overheard the two attending doctors discussing my disposition. They agreed no beds were available in the hospital. One attendant said, "No, leaving him in the hallway on a Gurney was not a p p r o p r i a . . ." The sedation had taken effect.

I had no idea how much time had elapsed, but the next thing I heard was a constant, intermittent beep, beep, beep, beep sound. I recognized the sound of a heart monitoring machine. It was exactly the same as one hears on television or in a movie theater. It meant my heart was still beating. The heart attack was not fatal; I was alive.

Even though still groggy from the sedative, I elevated my upper body, turning my head side to side, trying to determine where I was. Suddenly, I heard beeeeeeeeeeeeeeeeeep, a single, continuous, whining sound. I recalled this sound from television and it usually meant the heart stopped beating. Oh my G-d, my heart has stopped beating. I must be dead. One of the leads of the heart monitoring machine had come loose when I moved my body, but I did not know this. In my semiconscious state, I thought I was dead.

Startled, I jumped off the Gurney. I felt a painful, tearing sensation on several parts of my chest - the other EKG leads tearing away from my skin. I began running around the room, weaving in and out of the empty Gurneys shouting, "I'm dead.

I'm dead." I thought to myself, I've been so good, maybe a few indiscretions, but basically I've been so good. There is so much I want to do, so much I need to do, so many things I want to see. There are so many heights to climb and so many obstacles to overcome. Why did I die? Why am I dead? Dear G-d, why? I continued running up and down and around the Gurneys screaming, "I'm dead. I'm dead."

I did not know it at the time, but I had been placed in the intensive care unit (ICU). It was early afternoon and most of the patients had been sent to their respective rooms to recover from surgery, so space was available. Additionally, heart monitoring machines were readily available in this ward. In my sedated state, the many Gurneys in the room took on the appearance of horizontal tombstones. I could hear the sound of muffled guffaws, as though they were coming from the opening of a long tunnel. It appeared to be shaped like a doorway and was filled with laughing faces. Why were these faces laughing at me? Don't they realize I just died? They should be sad and upset. Yet, the laughter was getting louder and louder as more and more faces appeared in the opening.

As I looked around, the room appeared to resemble a hospital ward . . . it is a hospital ward. What's going on here? I was coming out of my sedated state and the room's objects were becoming less and less fuzzy. Those aren't tombstones, they are hospital beds. Those are real people standing in the doorway and laughing . . . and it is a doorway. Why are they laughing? They must be laughing at me. This crazy guy is running around the Gurneys in a half-opened hospital gown screaming about his death.

I finally figured it out. One of the leads of the heart monitoring machine must have come loose causing a break in the circuitry resulting in the long beeping sound. In my tranquilized state, I thought I died. In actuality, I was entertaining the staff running around the ward like a nut. Additionally, I was giving them a free, seminude show. With gowns designed to open in the back, I know why they call it ICU. I was grateful for one thing - I didn't see any flashbulbs go off but I was still mortified.

For the next three weeks, until I was discharged from the hospital, I was constantly smiled at by all the doctors and staff. I was the principal conversation piece of the entire hospital. While lying in bed, with plenty of time to reflect, I began to consider the possibility of my mortality.

I placed the immortality concept on hold, and one year after the heart attack my first book was published, followed soon after by full professorial rank at the dental college. Before retiring from teaching and private dental practice, I edited two books, wrote many articles, and lectured nationally and internationally. In my spare time, I was the President of two renown dental organizations and chaired a prestigious committee for the New York State Supreme Court, Appellate Division, First Department. Soon after my retirement, I published another book. Now seventy-seven years young, I am writing this, my third book. Having lived so long and accomplishing so much since my heart attack, the feeling of immortality is beginning to return. Why did I survive and what was I supposed to do with this gift? Ultimately, the answer to this question will surface. Perhaps I am being kept alive to finish my life's work, which needs defining. Time will tell.

I'D RATHER BE A HAS-BEEN
THAN A NEVER-WAS.

ANONYMOUS

TO KILL TIME IS NOT MURDER
IT'S SUICIDE.

WILLIAM JAMES

SEVEN

Midget

There is undeniable proof, derived from friends and relatives, that I measured six feet four inches tall in my stockinged feet on my wedding day.

After more than fifty years of marriage, I now stand five feet six inches tall when wearing shoes.

My wife strongly intimates that if we both are granted long life, I will die a midget.

DENIAL AIN'T JUST A RIVER IN EGYPT.

MARK TWAIN

**MEASURE A MAN'S ACCOMPLISHMENTS
BY THE OBSTACLES HE OVERCOMES
AND NOT
BY THE HEIGHTS HE ATTAINS.**

ANONYMOUS

EIGHT

The seasons

Situated on a rolling hillside in one of Long Island's premier neighborhoods, the house had considerable simplicity and charm. At its front, approximately eight feet below street level, a hand cut bluestone path and stairs led from the entrance to the street. The house was located across the road from the second highest point on Long Island. On a clear day, Connecticut was visible on the other side of Long Island Sound.

The builders who constructed this house wanted to maintain its rustic surrounding. They selectively cleared the site where the house, backyard and driveway were to be located and only removed trees that obstructed construction, thus maintaining its picturesque setting. Upon completion, the house was surrounded by tall oak trees, rhododendron, azaleas, and mountain laurel. The Cedar shake exterior of the house blended rustically with the natural, forested environment.

Set on three-quarters of an acre, the house encompassed thirty-seven hundred square feet of living space divided into three floors. Viewed from the front, the elevation appeared as a single level, ranch design. The main floor had three bedrooms and two-and-one-half baths. Additionally, there was a large entrance hallway, a family room, a large dining room, an eat-in kitchen, and a music room. Facing the rear of the house, the colonial facade was created by a raised roof which provided sufficient space in the upstairs level to allow for two full-sized bedrooms and a full sized bath. The lower floor contained a bedroom, a full bath, a small office, and sufficient space for a full sized pool table. Some purists might consider this lower floor a basement. However, the land's topographical features behind the house allowed for a sliding glass door entrance and windows. The area consisted of nine hundred square feet of space and it was light and airy making it more than a mere basement.

Walking through the family room to the rear of the house, a visitor passed a used-brick, wood-burning fire place and then exited through French doors onto a large, semicircular patio bordered by a used-brick wall. A concrete bench was embedded in this wall and a barbecue grill was located in the part of the wall that attached to the house's used-brick chimney. Cushions rested on the bench for soft seating. From the open side of the patio, a hand cut bluestone path led to bluestone stairs. Steps, lined at the sides with flowering ground cover, ended at a heart-shaped bluestone lower patio. Two stately oak trees stood at the site, each in a position corresponding to the left and right chambers of a heart. The patio was surrounded by grass and beyond the grass at the edge of the woods stood fifteen feet tall rhododendrons and azaleas with mountain laurel filling the spaces.

Spring

We were living in our house for more than two years when one spring evening my wife Bella said to me,

"You know what? We have a very large back yard and the

kids need something to do back there, something to play with so they can have the benefits of being outdoors. Furthermore, I would know exactly where they were because I can see them from the kitchen window."

She paused, her jaws tightened and with a deep breath, gasped,

"We should build a tree-house for the kids."

In woman talk, this means I should build the tree-house! It reminded me that marriage is a relationship in which one person is right and the other is the husband. I had just arrived home from work. It was 8:30 p.m. I was very tired; it had been a tough day at the office. I responded in a nasty, belligerent tone,

"Are you kidding? Do you see construction worker printed across my forehead? I'm too tired and don't want to talk about it."

Every night after this minor altercation, my wife, the kids, or both in conspiracy would gang-up on me and pursue the subject. Either singularly or in unison, they presented a litany of reasons why a tree-house was needed. Each declaration gave me more reason not to build it. On and on they went, night after night, until my resolve was shattered, my will broken. My wife's machinations demonstrated how she secured the Directorship of the C.I.A. (Certified Instigators Association). During my marriage I've learned there's only one way to handle a wife. Unfortunately, I haven't discovered what it is.

My devious Bella, sometimes called "she who must be obeyed," knew my limitations and that I would eventually succumb to pressure. Prior to her assault, she had already selected a site for the tree-house. In most families, husband and wife tend to think alike, with the wife having the last think. The moment I surrendered, she pointed out its location. Some wives never take part in an argument - they take all of it. Reluctantly, I agreed the choice was a good one. Four large oak trees sat off the edge of the grass at the back of the lower patio. Additionally, they were sufficiently close to each other to serve as a sound foundation for the tree-house.

What every do-it-yourself husband has is a do-it-now wife. I told my wife and kids that I would begin construction on the coming weekend but I would not set a date for its completion. It had to be built properly and be sturdy enough so no one would get hurt. I promised to draw up simple plans, secure the necessary materials, and then begin construction. I didn't want to kill myself so I estimated the project would take two to three weekends. After all, my avocation was not construction; I did not belong to the carpenter's union. Discounting the planning and purchasing of materials, the tree-house was actually completed in one day.

During the week, I developed the plan and determined the materials needed. All the basic tools were already in my possession. When the main house was being built, I saved left over lumber. I checked this cache, determined what was usable, and subtracted it from my previously determined needs. I now knew what to buy. On Saturday, determined that this tree-house would be a first class edifice, I went to the lumber yard and purchased everything needed. It would be sturdily built to prevent any accidents to my kids or their friends.

Early Sunday morning, I transported all the necessary tools and materials to the site and began construction. Supports were nailed to the inner surface of the foundation trees; a floor was nailed to these supports. Rather than just resting the plywood on the supports, I nailed everything together thus making the structure stronger for each side received some support from the reciprocal side.

I built a railing to prevent anyone from falling. The floor stood approximately seven feet above ground and a child could easily get hurt falling from this height. Since building an elevator would be overkill, I constructed a sturdy ladder that extended from the ground to the plywood floor. If my wife had been in charge of construction, toilet facilities and air conditioning would have been provided. A porta-potty was considered.

The finished structure was extremely sturdy. I was satisfied that my children and their friends would be safe. It was an architectural and engineering marvel worthy of designation as the eighth wonder of any father's world. In some circles, it would be comparable to the pyramids, and those required thousands of workers to build. Carpeting tacked to the tree-house floor and two chairs plus a small table gave it a homey feeling. It took a hard day's work to complete. However, when I watched my kids in the tree-house, it gave me a deep sense of accomplishment and enormous pleasure knowing my children had a new place to play. Bella, a very reliable source of gossip, learned from her neighborhood telephone contacts that my kids and their friends were enjoying the tree-house immensely. She had originated this excellent idea, schemed to get it, and thus deserved all the kudos. All things considered, it is usually the wife who has said it, and the husband who has done it.

Several weeks passed. After dinner one evening Bella, knowing I had a really good day at the office, said to me while tears rolled down her cheeks,

"Dear, I have terrible news." Whenever she used the term "dear" I knew it was going to be bad.

"What's the matter?" I replied in a concerned voice.

"Hold on to your chair," she said. Pausing, with an intense look on her face, she stammered, "the . . . tree-house . . . has . . . to be taken down."

I was holding on to my chair and still almost fell over. I was stunned. All the work and effort put into this project, in a noble cause, and it had to be undone? Life is not fair!

"Why?" I responded in a disbelieving tone.

"It seems there would be an insurance problem. If someone gets hurt, our insurance policy doesn't cover a tree-house." I wondered whether this was Miller's Law of Insurance where everything is covered except what happens? It sounded to me like some gossip down the street had planted this concern in her brain. Was the Pharaoh in Egypt worried about insurance for the Pyramids? Would he consider tearing them down because someone might get hurt?

"How the heck do you know?" I inquired. I don't mind not being the smartest person in the world, I just mind that someone else is - and that person might be my wife.

In a superior, know-it-all tone she replied, *"Because I called the insurance company."* The reason women usually win arguments with men is that only dumb men are foolish enough to argue with women.

That was a logical response. I was disappointed and upset but without question the tree-house had to come down. We did not need any legal problems. It would be dismantled the next weekend. I was not a happy camper.

My parents, who lived in Brooklyn, decided to visit me the day the tree-house was to be torn down. I did not expect the razing to take long so I did not stop them from visiting. They could watch me as I demolished my creation. I proceeded to knock down the railings using a sledge hammer because its extra weight made everything come apart easily.

My parents sat on the upper patio and watched the demise of the tree-house. They were shocked. They knew the structure was recently built and kept asking why it had to come down. They wanted to know why I didn't consider the insurance problem before it was built. They were concerned that my hands might be ruined or that I could get hurt in the deconstruction. A mother-in-law seldom seems to know where motherly love ends and meddling begins. "What is the matter with Bella? Doesn't she have anything better to do than create projects for you to waste your time?" My mother was annoyed. She sent her son to school to be a dentist not to be a carpenter. This confirmed her opinion that Bella was not the best choice for her special son.

I could not alleviate their concerns and their constant chatter was quite disconcerting. While they babbled, I worked on the plywood floor. Soon, it was lying on the grass. Finally, the steps came tumbling down and all that remained were the floor supports.

While dismantling the tree-house, I became increasingly upset. My status as a professional was compromised and my ego bruised. I was not schooled to be a carpenter. Why had I let my wife and kids talk me into doing this project? Why had I spent my valuable time building "Bella's Folly?" Now it had to be knocked down. Unfortunately, the kids had fun using it only for a short period. I was working myself into a rage, cussing and verbally abusing myself. I promised something like this would never happen again. I am always giving myself excellent advice, but I am incapable of taking it. By the time everything was removed, save the supports, I was fuming. Rage was an outlet for my frustration. My anger was beginning to distort my thinking. A vision of using the material to build a gallows to hang all the culprits who put me in this position crossed my mind. I would not even offer them the use of a blindfold. Well, perhaps an exception would be made for the little kids, but for Bella I would include a gag.

Now the remaining supports became the enemy that had to be destroyed. Angry and venting at one end of a support, I picked up the sledge hammer and with all my power took a mighty swing. "Damn you," I remarked as the sledge hammer made contact. "Pow," the hammer struck the end of the board. Unknowingly, this was a dumb decision. It was the wrong place to strike the first blow. In retaliation, the board immediately disengaged from the retainers on the struck end but the other end remained firmly attached to the tree. Acting like a spring, the end of the loosened support recoiled instantly, hitting the sledge hammer causing it to reverse direction and smashed me flush on my face. This reversal was pursuant to Newton's Third Law of Motion which states that, "for every action there is an equal and opposite reaction." It occurred so quickly, I really didn't know what happened. Stunned and semiconscious,

I stood momentarily immobile with blood flowing down my chin from a large split in my lip.

Quickly wheeling around, the sledge hammer firmly in my hand, I screamed loudly, "Who hit me? Where's the son-of-a-bitch who hit me? I'll kill him. Where is he?"

Dazed, I plunged to my knees and then onto the grass while continually looking for the cowardly, invisible man who struck me. Fortunately, the blow had hit me flush and no teeth were broken or knocked out - a dentist's luck.

Meanwhile, my parents hearing my screams began yelling for Bella. My wife ran out of the house and saw me laying on the ground, the sledge hammer still in my hand. I was moaning. She began screaming while running down the steps. Everyone was crying out except me. I was in "outer space" searching for the culprit who whacked me.

"What happened? What happened?" my wife shouted.

"I don't know. Someone hit me in the face." By now, blood covered most of my face and my shirt.

My wife searched for the culprit who hit me. Finally, she revealed that I had struck myself. A husband doesn't have to remember his own faults; his wife is sure to keep reminding him of them. Did I do this subconsciously as a form of self-punishment for my stupidity in starting this project?

"You're nuts. How could that have happened?" I mumbled.

She helped me up. I staggered to the upper patio. My parents were hysterical, especially my mother. She was infuriated because she felt Bella was responsible for the accident. A mother-in-law is the only law under which you are assumed to be guilty until proved innocent. My mother's rationale - it was Bella's idea to build the tree-house. Without this project there would be no construction and no injury to her cherished son. With a mother-in-law, there's nothing easier to find than fault, and nothing harder to keep than still. Mom always mistrusted Bella. The woman had taken me away from her protection when we married. A woman's mother-in-law is a relative, and

-48-

morally on her husband's side. My mother insisted I be taken to the hospital immediately. Bella sat me down on the wall bench, calmly took a wet towel and washed the blood from my face. The split lip was visible but the bleeding had slowed to an ooze. She decided there was no compelling reason to go to the emergency room. It would heal by itself.

Soon after, my parents departed visibly upset. They left assured of my continued existence, while my mother mumbled "Bella the . . . " The last word was not intelligible. My wife felt her mother-in-law slept with her glasses on, the better to see her daughter-in-law suffer in her dreams. I was physically and mentally drained from my bout with the tree-house and my fight with the invisible man. Worst of all, I had lost the fight. On the positive side, there would be a significant increase in my store of used lumber. Oh, joy! Looking at my wife and my children who had just arrived, I instinctively knew they were working on my next project. A few more undertakings like this one and my very survival would be in question.

Summer

It was the pain in my buttocks that convinced me something was afoot. A foot can be implanted in a buttock, but can a buttock be a foot? It was déjà vu, reminiscent of my Spring fiasco a couple of months earlier. The initial signal was the strange behavior of my children who appeared overly concerned with my health. It was extraordinary for them to constantly inquire if I was feeling O.K., and gratuitously undertaking my chores, like taking out the garbage. Subsequently, my wife started cooking my favorite foods more frequently and responding to my comments with, "yes, dear," and "certainly, dear." These adoring terms by consensual validation indicate the scheming woman wants something. It was obvious. They all wanted something, but what? A conspiracy was brewing.

One evening, when we were all sitting around the dinner table, I entreated my wife and kids,

"Okey! What's going on? Why are you all so solicitous?"

"What does sotilish . . . solatish . . . whatever that word was? What does it mean, Daddy?" inquired my five-year-old son.

"The word is pronounced so . . . lis . . . i . . . tus, and means showing interest or concern. For some reason, the entire family appears to be more concerned and interested in my needs than usual."

"But, we all love you," explained my son.

Aha, the little deceiver is part of the plot. Children are a great comfort in your old age, and they help you reach it faster. "Okey! Okey! That's enough. What is so important that you need a five-year-old shill as your spokesperson?" I quickly announced.

Suddenly, a menacing silence settled in the room. The children looked at each other then gazed at their mother. She reluctantly returned their stares. All eyes eventually focused on my wife who obviously was the chief conspirator. Nicknamed "The General" by my oldest son, it was obvious who orchestrated the conspiracy. The silence continued for a short time and then finally she spoke.

"What we need, *honey*," (it was the 'honey' attention getter), "what we need *desperately*" (the strong emphasis on 'desperately,' another attention getter), "is a dog run for Brandy."

"Oh my goodness," I cried. It is surprising that there aren't many more successful men - what with all the advice from their wives.

Brandy was an Old English Sheepdog, our family pet. These animals were originally bred in Great Britain to move and guard livestock. Brandy was a beautiful, thickset, muscular creature who was extremely active. She was shaggy, affectionate, perhaps a little dumb, but very lovable. The kids adored her. They could pull her, run into her, beat her up, pull the hair around her buttocks and she would not react, nor would she bark or make any other sound. Brandy was protective of her owners and was truly a great companion for the kids.

"Why the heck do you need a run for Brandy?" I inquired reasonably. "She meanders wherever she wants and never walks off the property. Right? In that respect, she is the best breed we ever had. Remember, she is a sheep-herding animal and knows our property's boundaries and where she can and cannot go." In a strident tone, I probed further. "Why do you want to shut her in a cage like an animal in a zoo?"

"Because there are problems when she needs to go outside," my wife quickly responded.

"What kind of problems?"

"There are times she needs to be walked and no one is available to walk her. She is so large the younger kids cannot handle her. Sometimes, I'm unavailable. If I let her loose, she occasionally goes into the woods. I know that's still our property but she picks up little crawly bugs on her coat, especially ticks and brings them into the house. You know that's already happened. If we had a run all that could be prevented." This was my wife's Aristotelian argument, on the surface quite logical, but really deeply flawed. Brandy still would have to be walked to the run where she could pick up those little crawly things during the trip or while in the run. Husbands have more problems than wives - for one thing, they have to put up with wives.

I looked at my wife for a moment, then looked at the kids and inquired in a sarcastic tone, "I suppose you guys have already picked out the site for this desperately needed run?"

They nodded simultaneously, further justifying my suspicion that I was a pawn in a Machiavellian plot.

"Yes," acknowledged Bella. "I would build it on the side of the house near the sliding glass door entrance to the lower level." The incomparable manipulator then added, "But, if you can think of a better place for it dear, we can discuss it further." A man can't win an argument with his wife, but he can break even by keeping his mouth shut.

Bella was becoming extremely emotional. She had owned and loved animals since childhood and was very protective of them. I was certain that if my wife had to choose between me and Brandy I was expendable.

It all began when she was six years old and her father brought home a mixed breed, Spitz- Collie and named Poochie. She was a remarkable animal, a wonderful pet and a great guard dog. When she barked, the walls shook. This dog was treated more like a human being than an animal. She ate the same food as the family and never dog food. Occasionally, she was given biscuits to help clean her teeth. Poochie perfected one of life's secret lessons that if you stare hard and long enough at someone, eventually you will get what you want. The dog's primary treat or dessert was one bagel every day (no butter, no cream cheese, no lox). She and my wife had a wonderful relationship for many years, but unfortunately Brandy died shortly after Bella and I married.

Poochie was the first animal Bella owned. Afterwards, she (we) owned a Boxer, a Golden Retriever, two Irish Setters, a Scottish Sheepdog, Brandy and a partridge in a pear tree. All were pure breeds. Whenever the time came to select a breed, my wife and I had an equal vote. It was understood that my wife's vote was more equal than mine. My wife liked all kinds of dogs and felt the Old English Sheepdog was the best. Brandy was her favorite.

My wife is a very special person. Being a husband is like any other job - it helps if you like the boss and remember that the views expressed by husbands at home are not necessarily those of the management. However, I had not forgotten the tree-house fiasco. Would this dog run eventually have to be torn down because of some city ordinance? What about insurance? What was the possibility of me getting hurt during its construction? Realizing my physical limitations and mental deficiency when doing construction, anything could happen. I was concerned about Gattuso's extension of Murphy's Law: "that nothing

-52-

is never so bad that it cannot get worse." But, evaluating the strong arguments my family presented and the highly emotional involvement of everyone, how could their request be refused?

Finally, I grudgingly agreed but on certain strict conditions, namely "that you are certain there are no laws against building a dog run and there are no insurance problems. I expect you to research this thoroughly then I will build it for you. But I know nothing about building a dog run so I will have to do some research. When I have enough information, I will build it. In other words, stay out of my face, and it will be finished when it is finished. And it doesn't depend upon a singing fat lady. In fact, there isn't one in town." I paused for a moment, and then continued, "Do we have an agreement?"

The profound silence in the room was a sufficient answer.

Outside the basement's sliding glass doors was a concrete slab and on either side of this slab stood concrete retaining walls. The wall on the side nearest the woods was relatively low, perhaps three feet high. I intended to build the dog run between the embankment created by this wall and the woods. The ground was flat: it was out of the way and very accessible from the basement. During inclement weather, it would not create too much of an inconvenience going from the basement's exit to the dog run.

I had no clue about building a dog run but over the years I was involved in different construction projects. The nine hundred square foot basement (lower level) was finished with my oldest son's help. We dropped the ceiling, fabricated Tudor-style walls with stucco, and installed all the electrical work including the fixtures and outlets. My son and I also constructed a full-bath. We built the room, tiled the floor, painted and papered the walls, and installed the cabinets. The toilet, sink, shower, and pump were not done by us. Those were installed by a plumber. We also built closets, stained woodwork and installed dado walls, all to my wife's satisfaction, a demanding taskmaster. She approved the results so my performance could not have been too bad. But I never built a dog run.

John was the person for advice. He was the manager of our local lumber yard and was very knowledgeable about most construction projects. Over the years, I befriended John and knew he would have the necessary information. John had several ideas and we formulated a simple, inexpensive plan to build the run. I not only use all the brains I have, but all that I can borrow. Galvanized steel would be employed for the project because wood tends to rot and decay.

Brandy was not aggressive, therefore, chicken wire would be used for the fence instead of chain links. It is less expensive, sufficiently strong to contain the animal, easy to work with and it keeps small creatures out. The wire is attached to corrugated, galvanized steel poles that are pounded into the ground. John suggested a prefabricated gate constructed of galvanized pipe, set into concrete footings. The run would be rectangular in shape and the right-angled corners would reinforce its sturdiness. The dog run would be fifteen feet long by five feet wide. This would fit in the available space and it appeared sufficient. I purchased the materials and it was delivered to my home the next day.

It is a good idea to patronize a single store for all your needs. This helps establish a rapport with the owner or manager and often results in some discount or perk. This strategy paid off when John said he would not charge me for his pole setter. This heavy piece of equipment looks like a large, circumferential, steel pipe with handles on opposite sides and one end closed off. It is used by placing the open end over a pole and then bringing it down forcefully, thus hammering the pole into the ground.

I began construction early on a Saturday morning. With my oldest son's help, the upright supports of the gate were placed into excavations. These foundation holes were filled with concrete. After the concrete hardened and the gate was sturdy, we were ready to erect the fence. At this point, the project looked bizarre, a gate standing alone that anyone could walk through on their way to nowhere.

The following morning, we started to erect the fence. Poles were placed at predetermined intervals. Each pole was set into the ground by hand as deeply as possible. After placing all the poles, it was time to use the pole setter.

Initially, with a few forceful, downward thrusts each pole seemed to go into the ground rather easily. As the pole setting progressed, it became more and more difficult. Either the ground was getting harder or I was getting tired. In either case, it felt like I was working like a dog.

My arms began to ache as I continued banging the poles. As my arms tired, the pole setter was lifted higher and higher to help increase the resultant downward thrust. I should have stopped, but stubbornly continued. I began to lose control of the pole setter. I raised the setter too high and when bringing it downward, missed the pole and the setter came down on my head.

Again, my head was used for an unintended purpose. Sledge hammer, pole setter, it made no difference. At least my hard head had some value. It was another act of stupidity. Perhaps it explains why people say I am brainless. It was another knockout blow.

Nobody knows how long my body laid prostrate on the ground. I vaguely recall my son asking if I was doing all right. Supposedly, my response was "I make a living." My son's official report to my wife disclosed that I was unconscious and prostrate for two to three minutes. She no longer had confidence in my abilities as a construction worker. The faults of wives are many, husbands have only two - everything they say, and everything they do.

This time my wife wanted to take me to the hospital. To avoid this, I rose quickly and continued working on the dog run. With my head pounding, I resumed pounding the poles in concert vowing not to leave this project unfinished, even if it killed me. It almost did!

With a great deal of temerity and caution, the last few poles were set. The chicken wire was connected to the poles and the gate, completing the dog run. One of the kids ran to get Brandy. Initially, she did not want to go into the "cage." Clearly, on some high level of dog consciousness, she recognized that it would restrict her freedom. She probably understood that the life she previously led was better. I totally understood. Finally, she entered the "edifice" and looked around. Her face had a wondering look: was the cage to keep her in or us out?

The dog run was used for exactly one entire week. This time, its lack of use was not a potential insurance problem nor a violation of a city ordinance. My wife and children found it easier to let Brandy run loose rather than take her to and from the enclosure. Suddenly their concern with ticks and bugs was unimportant. The sole advantage was the cage made it easier to find Brandy's deposits when she banked them in the run.

The dog run stood idle for a few months until one of my brilliant kids figured out it could be used to hold ducks, rabbits, and other cageable pets. Just as the tree house was demolished in the spring, the dog run was relegated to the summer's dust heap of intended purposes.

Fall

The resumption of school for the children marked the beginning of fall at our home. My wife once confided to me that her emancipation occurred the day her youngest child began attending school. She could then food shop and do errands without dragging one or more of the kids along. It was about having time for herself. As the mother of young children, there's a time and place for everything except rest. Bella would often remark that there is nothing like the joy of motherhood, especially when all the children are in bed.

"She who roars the loudest" preferred to not have a kitchen at all - only vending machines. But, our home did have a very large eat-in kitchen containing custom-built, solid oak cabinets. Conspicuous among these cabinets was a large double oven. Because my wife is short, she exaggerated the truth when she claimed to be five feet three-quarters of an inch tall, the oven was placed closer to the floor than usual to facilitate her access. This resulted in a very tall cabinet above the oven and a very narrow cabinet below. Mrs. Hardworker wanted to put a sign on the cabinet above the oven that read, "kitchen closed because of illness - I'm sick of cooking," but I put my foot down and vetoed the request. When you win an argument with your wife, the argument is not necessarily over. A step stool was necessary for her to reach the upper cabinet. Furthermore, she needed to be on her knees to gain access to the lower one, a position she never would assume. This lower cabinet was never used, or so we believed.

The round table was another of Bella's time saving ideas. It was a thoughtful one. She felt the table would be sufficient for meals and it would also help her manage the children's homework. This proved to be true. They were in different grades and their tutoring needs differed. My very bright children loved the round table rather than a square or rectangular one. The kids believed that if they did something wrong they could not be cornered with a round table. What brilliance! With a round table, "the boss" could "circle the wagons" and assist the children with their specific class needs without the kids moving. The children knew that if they did not cooperate and concentrate on their home work they would suffer "the slings and arrows" of terrible misfortune. My wife, the "General," had a motto; to err is human, but to forget is unlikely. The setting was comparable to a one room school house and teaching the kids at their different class levels worked advantageously. Otherwise, each child would have to chase after the "General" or she would have to visit each child's room. In either case, it would waste a great deal of time and energy.

It was at this table, during a study interlude, that my youngest son asked my wife a family pedigree-type question.

"Mom, where did you meet Dad?"

"In a bowling alley on Veterans Day," she replied.

"What is Veterans Day?" he questioned further.

"Veterans Day used to be called Armistice Day and commemorates the day World War I ended. It falls on November 11 each year. The name was changed to represent all the people who have fought and defended our country. You know, like soldiers and sailors," she responded.

"What does commemorates mean?" he shot back.

"It means . . . like . . . celebrates," my wife explained.

Our son stared at his mother, paused, and declared,

"Do you mean that on Veterans Day, a day that celebrates fighting people, you met Dad at the bowling alley? Mom, did you know that each alley has a return button for the pins and balls? Are you trying to tell me that when you first met Dad you had the opportunity to press the return button and didn't?" My wife looked bewildered for a moment, and then burst out laughing. All the other kids joined in.

The one thing the kids never had to do was say a prayer before a meal because Mom was a great cook. After breakfast one morning, my wife followed her usual routine. She bundled all the kids off to school, cleaned the kitchen, and did some light housekeeping. She had to go shopping, so she dressed and left the house about ten a.m.

When she returned, it was nearly one p.m. She pulled into the garage, closed its door, and proceeded to empty the car of the spoils of shopping. There were only three bundles but one was quite large. Nevertheless, she decided to take all three packages to avoid making a second trip. The large package partially blocked her vision, but she managed to maneuver through the mud-room, through the kitchen and family room, and into the master bedroom. The size of the parcels prevented her from noticing the broken glass on the mud room floor. She did notice the door to the lower level (basement) was slightly ajar. Can a door be a jar? Anxious to put away the parcels, she did not think about it.

She walked into the bedroom and was abruptly startled. Most of the dresser drawers and closet doors were open, their contents strewn all over the floor and bed. The mattress was lying partially on the floor.

She wondered if the kids came home early from school and were responsible for this destruction? Not likely. She would have seen or heard them if they were in the house. Suddenly, my wife remembered the door that was ajar, and recalled that recently, several burglaries had occurred in the neighborhood. Perhaps this was another one? She went back to the family room, walked to the fireplace, picked up a log, and returned to the door. She held the log high over her head in the warrior's assault position. Stretched, my wife was slightly more than five feet tall and with a log two feet long she became a seven-foot monster. She had made a conscious decision, if not an unwise one, to protect her home. Let the intruder beware! I can imagine what would have happened if a big, muscular, burglar bounded up the basement stairs. I can see the determined look on my wife's face. Her killing stare would have immobilized the intruder and stopped him in his tracks. She would have hospitalized this stranger with a mighty swing of the log followed by several nasty left hooks. Her sons could testify to the severity and punishing nature of these blows; I shudder at the thought. She paused at the door for a moment, listening for any unusual sound coming from below then shouted slowly and loudly,

"I'm now . . . going . . . to call . . . the police . . . You better . . . get out . . . while you can."

After this declaration, she nonchalantly walked into the kitchen, picked up the phone, then walked into the mud room.

She noticed the broken glass for the first time, immediately closed the door, and dialed 911.

"I'm on the phone right now with the police. You better get out of here," the little warrior once again shouted loudly while facing the ceiling vent above. This vent was often used as a substitute megaphone when calling the children to come downstairs. The police arrived about fifteen minutes later.

At a little past three p.m., our youngest child, Ben, returned home from school. He did not recognize the two cars parked in the driveway and when he walked into the house asked my wife to whom they belonged?

"Detectives," she replied sadly, "we've been robbed."

At that moment, Ben noticed three unfamiliar men. He assumed they were the detectives for they marched around the house brushing stuff on the walls and door knobs while continually interrogating my wife. "What time did you leave the house? What time did you return? Can you tell if anything is missing? What is your age?" This question puzzled my wife. She inquired why was her age important? When they replied that it was for statistical purposes, she refused to answer. During this entire time, my son remained in the background, quietly observing the actions of the detectives.

At roughly four p.m., the detectives left. My wife was very anxious and nervous. She is great during an emergency, but often falls apart afterward. My eight-year-old son walked with her into the kitchen and tried to console her. He brought her a glass of iced tea and inquired,

"So what really happened, Mom?"

"Like I said before, we've been robbed," my wife responded. She paused for a moment to take a drink. "Apparently, they broke the glass on the mud room door to gain access to the doorknob and that's how they got in. Then they ransacked the house. They went upstairs in your sister's bedroom and into your bedroom looking for money, jewelry, or anything valuable."

With a quizzical look on his face, Ben asked,

"Did they take anything?"

"Well, first of all," my wife replied, "the most important thing is nobody was hurt and they didn't destroy anything. If you remember, Mrs. Lipnicki was burglarized last month and the robbers destroyed her house. They ripped the bed linens and dirtied her drapes and carpeting. Thank goodness they didn't do that here. As far as I can tell, they took a bracelet of mine from my dresser drawer and a few of your sister's bracelets. None was worth a lot of money but they had sentimental value. They found no cash because your father and I never leave any lying around. Our money is always used to pay bills so we have no cash to hide in the house."

With that comment, Ben's eyes opened wide furrowing his forehead. He became pale as the blood drained from his face. He took two short, quick steps and then slid on his stomach across the kitchen until he reached the narrow cabinet beneath the double oven. He opened the door and took out a jar that jingled. Rising from the floor, he held the jar high above his head, shook it heartily and began to laugh as though the victor in some important contest. The jar was full of coins.

Having the last laugh he screamed, "Yippee, they didn't get my money." It was as if he understood that a grown person would never stoop that low to look for something.

The jar contained all the money he had earned doing chores over the past few months. Who cares whether a door is ajar as long as the jar remains full of coins.

Winter

Winters on rustic rolling hills tend to be spectacular, especially when it snows. However, snow creates several problems. Snow covering steep roadways made getting to my home atop a hill difficult. It often precluded me reaching home until the streets were plowed and sanded. Going down the hills also proved to be an adventure. When the road was icy, using the car's brakes to control movement was very treacherous often causing the car to skid.

My garage doors were eight feet below street level at the end of a fifty-foot long slope. These doors had been assaulted numerous times as cars skidded down our snowy, icy driveway. The broken garage doors stood as a reminder of the difficulty of stopping a moving car on an icy slope. I could have installed metal barriers to protect the doors, but it would have been costly. If our car was in the garage prior to a snow storm, it was impossible to get the car to the street level. In this position, the rear-end traction was insufficient to move the car up the driveway's incline.

My wife, the leader of the pack, once tried to back the car out of the garage after a storm. She got halfway up the slope and the wheels began spinning. Realizing she could go no further, she stepped on the brakes but the car just slid back down the slope smashing into the garage. She knew that all the snow and ice had to be removed and the driveway well salted before she could back out, nevertheless she tried it with disastrous results. My wife knew I hated salt in my food so she never used salt when cooking. Perhaps she thought a salt-free driveway was the answer. To avoid the problem, we would park the car at the top of the driveway at street level before the storm. But if the snowfall was heavy, we would have to clean the car. Clearly, a disadvantage in not sheltering the car in the garage.

We became weather watchers, carefully monitoring weather reports. When snow was predicted, we backed the car into the garage. With the car's wheels at the back of the garage, we found we could get sufficient traction from the dry, eighteen foot long floor. This "running start" allowed us to move the car up to the street level. This was a potentially treacherous procedure because it was extremely difficult to stop the car's forward movement at the top of the driveway. If another car came along at the wrong moment, a disastrous collision could have occurred. Fortunately, we lived in our house for twenty-one winters and no such accident happened.

There were benefits that compensated for the disadvantages of winter driving. Our home, located on three-quarters of an acre, was beautiful when covered with a layer of snow. The wooded areas were primarily stately oak trees. When oak trees lose their leaves in the winter, the snow piles high on the empty branches and creates a stunning scene of majestic white. On cold, sunny days, light breaks into prismatic colors that haloes the trees. Snow mantles the rhododendron and mountain laurel at the base of these oaks, creating the illusion of a white carpet studded in green.

Besides its beauty, the snow allows for winter sports. Our property has a continuous pitch to the woods behind the house ending approximately fifteen feet below street level. On the side of the house, there is sufficient space between the woods and the garage to create a continuous, unobstructed slope of almost two hundred feet. We had no lift so skiing would be difficult, but we soon discovered it made for great sledding. On several occasions, we hooked-up our old English sheepdog to the sled. The dog was not delighted pulling the sled but the kids thought it was great fun.

With a modest thickness of snow on the ground, we could take a sled, get a running start at the street level and down the driveway we would go. We would maneuver around the edge of the garage onto the snow-covered grass and end at the edge of the wooded area. It was great fun and my children and I would take turns going down the slope. Upon reaching the bottom, one of the kids would always be asked to take the sled back to the top. Various infirmities were employed, such as weakness, fatigue and even old age as excuses to avoid dragging the sled back up the hill. My bottom line reason was it would be their turn next. My mother did not raise a dummy. When I was a child, the best sled to own was a Flexible Flyer. They are still being manufactured. These sleds come in various lengths: short, medium, and long. Since my children were relatively little, a small one was bought. A grown person could use this sled by keeping the lower part of his legs in a bent position while going down the hill. Later, a more comfortable, medium sized sled was purchased for me.

The Flexible Flyer is made from hardwood slats attached to steel runners. The front part of the runners is attached to a piece of hardwood that is shaped like a bicycle's handlebar. Pushing or pulling the ends of this hardwood bar makes the runners turn to the left or right causing the sled to turn in a corresponding direction. It is relatively easy to do. The sled can make a significant turn depending upon the strength of the sledder and the distance the handlebar can be moved. One unique advantage is while sitting the sledder can hold onto a narrow slat on each side and steer with his feet, alternately pushing the left or right side of the handlebar. Flexible Flyer sleds have side attachments for smaller children. This gives the child heightened stability and security, minimizing the possibility of falling off. Each end of the handlebar has a hole through which a rope can be attached. Instead of using his feet, a child can steer by alternately pulling on the rope. After finishing a run, the rope can be used to pull the sled to the top of the slope. Older children can lift the sled over their heads and in this manner return the sled to the starting area for the next sledder.

The older children and adults eventually moved on to the "belly-whopping" stage. This is an advanced technique that requires a reasonable amount of athletic skill. The sledder grasps the sled with both hands and holds it diagonally across his body. He concludes the running start (the length and quickness of the run determine the eventual speed of the sled down the slope) by leaping off his feet while holding the sled and landing on top of the sled the instant it hits the snow. This creates considerable momentum going down the slope and increases the sledder's "rush." The sled run passes quicker but the euphoria is well worth it. Of course, the faster you go down the slope the greater the possibility of falling off. At least one member of the family was always cut or bruised from an errant ride. Avoiding obstacles such as trees or the house becomes more difficult as the speed increases. Additionally, an increase in speed causes a decrease in reaction time. Hitting the house or a tree was one method of reducing speed. This happened occasionally. Fortunately, we never broke any bones.

One magnificent Sunday morning we awoke to a thick, beautiful blanket of snow covering the landscape. The snow had fallen throughout the night, covering the ground and clinging to the trees. What a marvelous sight!

It was time for sledding. It was bitter cold; however, the sun's rays warmed your face. The kids and I were on our special, private sled run. It snowed heavily two days earlier and the sled path was deep and tightly packed. The new snow made sledding better and we went down the slope repeatedly. We had been sledding in the cold for over an hour and were looking forward to a good lunch, perhaps a hot cup of soup with a sandwich, and finally "chilling out" in front of a roaring fire. I could taste Cognac on my lips.

A car came up the plowed, well-sanded road. I immediately recognized my brother's car. He stopped the car near my driveway, jumped out, ran up to me and in a childlike fashion asked,

"What are you guys doing?"

It appeared rather obvious, but I replied affectionately,

"We're sledding, dummy. Can't you tell?"

"Wow. I haven't done that in years," my brother replied. "When can I have a turn?"

At the time, my brother was in his middle thirties. I was certain he had not been on a sled for at least the past twenty years. Furthermore, he was not an athletic person. Devoted to cerebral activities, his prowess on a sled was minimal at best.

"Peter, it's a rather steep hill and you haven't been on a sled in years," I counseled, "it could be dangerous. I don't want you to get hurt so why don't you take one of the sleds and practice at the bottom of the hill before you take the long run from street level."

"Come on, give me a break," he replied. "It's no big deal. You don't have to be an Olympic slalom medalist to go down a hill on a sled. If the kids can do it, I certainly can do it."

Peter is my younger brother; there is a five-year difference in our ages. He can be rather stubborn. His wife Joan was standing nearby. They had recently married and I really didn't want to take on the "older brother" attitude in front of her. But I distrusted his ability to "belly-whop." I was worried about his safety. At the beginning of the run, if he didn't steer appropriately at the right moment, he could run into the garage door or a tree.

He remained adamant. While watching the kids go down the slope, he assured me several times that steering would not be a problem. You could sense he was visualizing in his mind how to hold the sled while noting the necessary running start and the required leap onto the driveway. After a few minutes he said to me,

"Which sled should I use?"

My brother is five feet, ten inches tall. I suggested he use the larger sled. The smaller sled would not provide enough support for him even if he were able to control the lower part of his legs.

"O.K.," he said, impatiently. "Give me the sled and watch out. Let's do it."

My brother took the sled and walked across the street. You could see him fingering the sled, trying to determine the best place to grasp for proper balance. He stood there for a few moments, looked to his left and then to his right to make sure there were no cars coming. Then he started his run. My brother has long legs and it only took a few strides for him to reach the release point at the top of the driveway. He leaped . . . and I could not believe what followed. He seemed to freeze for several seconds at the top of his leap and then all of a sudden he let go of the sled while erupting with a horrible, chilling scream,

"Oooohhh . . . mmmyyyyy . . . GGGGoooodddd."

My brother landed on his stomach and slid down the icy driveway on his belly. Meanwhile, the sled went down the slope, disappearing behind the garage as my brother continued his descent down the driveway.

It was the funniest thing I had ever seen, the sled flying in one direction and my brother in the other. I was hysterical. I laughed so hard the tears froze on my face. Suddenly, my laughter turned to grave concern. My brother was sliding down the ice-slickened driveway and would inevitably hit the garage door. It seemed like a millennium, but it probably took only a few seconds for him to traverse fifty feet. Then it happened. I heard a very loud "baaaam" when my brother's head hit the garage door. He just lay there limp and for a moment I thought he was dead. He started to move slightly and began to groan. Holy Cow! I thought, how badly is he hurt? In spite of the icy driveway I ran to him and shouted,

"Peter, Peter are you O.K.?"

"What happened? What happened?" my brother asked as he slowly rolled over. He was severely jolted but not hurt.

"You just gave us an outstanding demonstration of the true meaning of the word 'belly-whopping'."

EITHER YOU'RE FAST OR YOU'RE FANCY. IT'S TOUGH TO BE BOTH AT THE SAME TIME.

THE AUTHOR

**THE FUTURE BELONGS TO THOSE
WHO BELIEVE
IN THE BEAUTY OF THEIR DREAMS.**

ELEANOR ROOSEVELT

**A BABY IS GOD'S OPINION THAT THE
WORLD SHOULD GO ON.**

CARL SANDBERG

NINE

Jake

His given name was Marvin, but he was always called Jake. Crowned with this nickname in early childhood, no one could recall its origin. Jake was my wife's favorite uncle. They were devoted to each other. My wife's affection began at an early age and grew deeply while her uncle served in the United States Army during World War II.

In October 1940, the Burke-Wadsworth Act was enacted creating the first peacetime draft in the history of the United States. Men between the ages of twenty-five to thirty-five had to register for this draft. Through a lottery system, men were selected for military service not to exceed twelve months. In the summer of 1941, Congress extended the term of duty beyond twelve months. After the United States entered World War II, termination of service was extended to six months after the war's end.

Jake was in his early thirties in November 1940 when he was one of the first to be selected in this lottery. He went through basic training and then was assigned to be a cook. Jake had no particular training as a cook and did not want to be a cook. But when selecting someone predicated on talent, there is the right way, the wrong way, and the Army way.

December 7, 1941 marked the beginning of World War II. Jake was a Corporal. My wife began writing letters to him, and he would respond from where he was stationed. Jake was constantly cooking while my wife constantly corresponded with him. Jake was discharged in December 1945 a Master Sargent.

After his release from the Army, Jake returned to his former civilian occupation working as a carpet and tile installer for his brother-in-law's company. He was a quiet, affable person with a great sense of humor. You could kid with Jake and he would dish it right back. He was fun to be with and I certainly understood why he was my wife's favorite uncle.

After my wife and I married in 1953, I noticed that my wife constantly asked Uncle Jake for one of his Army recipes. He was supposedly a very good cook and once prepared a meal for General Eisenhower. She would ask Jake for a recipe every time they were together and each time he would refuse.

"Listen, I love you," he would exclaim, "but I cooked three meals a day for more than five years and I don't want to think about cooking. It's bad enough I have to cook for myself." Jake was a bachelor.

Time and time again, my wife would ask him for one of his recipes and each time her request was emphatically denied. This repartee went on for years, to the point that when meeting my wife, he would begin his salutation by saying,

"No recipe today! How are you doing my darling?"

One day my wife responded to this greeting.

"Uncle Jake, I love you and want you to live until you're one hundred and twenty. You are presently seventy-five, so that leaves me only forty-five more years to wangle a recipe from you. Why don't you give me one recipe and we can avoid this banter forevermore? What do you say? Can I have just one recipe? Please!"

Jake eyed her sternly, hesitated for a moment, and responded, "Let's make a deal. If you assure me you will never again ask, I'll give you one recipe, but you have to promise. Deal?"

My wife looked at him with a big grin, like she had worn him down and won the battle. "I promise Uncle Jake," my wife replied, "one recipe and I'll never bother you again." "O.K.," Jake shot back, "one recipe and never again will you pester me. That's the deal. Now go get a pencil and a large piece of paper."

My wife scurried around excitedly, looking for pencil and paper. Finally finding what she needed, she sat down. With a smile on her face and exaltation in her voice she emphatically pronounced,

"I'm ready."

"You're sure you're ready?" Jake inquired. "I don't want to have to repeat myself." He was milking it for all it was worth.

"I'm ready," my wife pronounced decidedly, her eyes glued to the piece of paper in front of her.

"O.K. here goes," Jake announced. "This recipe is for a stew I made several times a week for the battalion. Don't miss any ingredients." He paused. "Take seven hundred pounds of potting meat and nine hundred pounds of potatoes . . . "

My wife began writing and suddenly she stopped and her lower jaw dropped open. She looked up with a startled, dumbfounded expression on her face and exclaimed,

"Wait a minute. What are you talking about? What do you mean seven hundred pounds of potting meat and nine hundred pounds of potatoes? I don't understand."

"That's because you are a dumbbell, but I still love you," he announced. "You want something but you don't think about what you want. For years you have asked me for a recipe. But

I cooked for thousands of soldiers at a time. I don't know any recipes for a small number of people."

My wife was perplexed and terribly disappointed. We all had a good laugh at her expense. She took it like a good sport. We were all reminded that wishing can result in unintended consequences.

**I AM NOT AFRAID OF DEATH.
WHAT I FEAR
IS LIFE WITHOUT INTEREST.**

ANONYMOUS

**SOMETIMES YOU'RE THE PIGEON
AND SOMETIMES YOU'RE THE STATUE.**

ANONYMOUS

TEN

Twofer

Married friends who have the same first names are remarkably rare. Sam and Bella. Bella and Sam. The names were interchangeable and our friendship close. When we went out to dinner together, two heads always turned when one name was called.

Unfortunately, my namesake passed away at an early age. My wife and I remained close friends with Bella despite the tragedy. We often took her to dinner, reminiscing over the wonderful times our friendship produced.

On one occasion, my wife and I took Bella to a local Japanese restaurant. We spoke with Bella on the telephone regularly, and went to dinner with her as often as possible. These meetings, though infrequent, were always full of frivolity and our time together passed quickly.

When we went out to eat, I usually sat between both Bellas. On one occasion, I noticed the waiter constantly watching us. After awhile, I called the waiter over to our table and asked if anything was wrong.

"Ah, so," he responded in his Japanese-English dialect. "Evlyting O.K." He bowed in our direction and remained standing at the table side.

"But you have been staring at us all evening. Why?" I questioned him again.

"Two ruvry rady, one man, vely nice. I rike, I watch," he replied and then walked away.

As dinner progressed, the waiter continued to watch us. As he served the dessert, I reminded him that he was still watching us intently. "Are these ladies so beautiful that you cannot stop looking at them?" The waiter had no choice but to answer this question in the affirmative. It was a wonderful way to manufacture a compliment for my two Bellas.

"Yes," acknowledged the waiter, confirming my theory. "Orso notice both rady name Berra," he added.

So! He was both watching us and listening to our conversation. I also knew he was not referring to Yogi Berra, the former baseball player.

"There is a reason both ladies are named Bella," I continued. "Would you like to know why?"

"Ah, so, vely intelesting," he replied, bowing once again as he spoke.

"This lady, I pointed to my right, is my wife and this lady, pointing to my left, is my mistress."

The waiter's eyes widened considerably and again he bowed while emitting a long, surprised, "Ahhhh . . . Soooo."

"They have the same name so whenever I sleep with one of them and if I should call out the name Bella in my dream, neither will know which one I mean. Therefore, one will not become jealous of the other and they both remain satisfied and happy."

"You . . . one . . . rucky . . . ferra," the waiter said slowly and cheerfully. He had a big smile on his face and bowed deeply, an expression of considerable respect.

"I no burrashitsu," I responded in his language.

BUT WHAT IS HAPPINESS EXCEPT THE SIMPLE HARMONY BETWEEN A MAN AND THE LIFE HE LEADS.

ALBERT CAMUS

IF YOU DON'T STAND FOR SOMETHING YOU'LL FALL FOR ANYTHING.

ANONYMOUS

**NEITHER SUCCESS NOR FAILURE
IS NECESSARILY FINAL.**

ANONYMOUS

**THE CHURCH IS NEARBY,
BUT THE ROAD IS ICY.
THE BAR IS FAR AWAY . . .
SO I'LL WALK CAREFULLY.**

RUSSIAN PROVERB

ELEVEN

A signature tale

A pronounced buzz reverberated throughout the office. Everybody was talking with each other but none could exceed the verbosity of the receptionist. After all, isn't the ability to speak the primary criterion for a good receptionist? The buzz, however, extended beyond normal conversation and gossip. It is especially difficult to keep a secret in a small office, though there was no particular reason to keep this information confidential. The truth is, this secret needed to be shouted from the rooftops. *Joltin' Joe DiMaggio is coming to my office to have his teeth cleaned.* The Yankee Clipper, . . . baseball icon, . . . former husband of Marilyn Monroe, . . . member of the Baseball Hall of Fame, . . . and one of the most famous persons in the United States.

I was in the midst of treating a patient who commuted from his home in Las Vegas to my office in New York. Las Vegas was also Joe DiMaggio's hometown, and they were friends. One day, my patient asked if I would clean Mr. DiMaggio's teeth. He was going to be in New York and I was chosen his "teeth cleaner." What a thrill this would be for me. I was born and brought up in Brooklyn, New York and was a die hard Brooklyn Dodgers baseball fan until they moved to California in 1957 and became the Los Angeles Dodgers. I then became a New York Yankee fan. Joe DiMaggio was a legend among legendary Yankee baseball players. Of course, the cleaning was expected to be "on the cuff," a freebie. For Joe DiMaggio, why not?

My patient made an appointment for Joe and I couldn't resist telling my patients, or anyone else that would listen, that Joe DiMaggio is coming to my office. This type of information should not be kept confidential and was the main reason for the extraordinary buzz going around the office. It was early in my career and spreading the news that Jolten' Joe is my patient would be a practice builder. Also, it would undoubtedly boost my ego.

Movie and Broadway luminaries among my patients often did not show up on their appointed day or came late. They assumed their celebrity status gave them special privileges. But Joe DiMaggio, bigger than life, entered my office on time. My receptionist, with a big, welcoming smile, greeted him warmly. She was a Yankee fan too.

"Good morning Mr. DiMaggio," my receptionist softly said, extending her hand so Joe could take the document she was holding. "This is our health questionnaire and I would appreciate it if you would fill it out."

Mr. DiMaggio took the questionnaire, looked at it for a moment, and his eyebrows elevated causing furrows to cross his forehead. He handed it back, gave her a curious look and politely said,

"No thanks."

Without another word, he turned around and walked out of the office.

The entire staff was watching and when Mr. DiMaggio

departed everyone was astonished. If a pin had dropped on the floor, the resonance would have been deafening. Everyone was dismayed and no one had a plausible explanation for his abrupt behavior.

I immediately picked up a phone and placed a call to my patient in Las Vegas who referred Mr. DiMaggio. I explained the circumstances and he had no explanation. He did mention that Joe was often temperamental and maybe he was having a bad day. We chalked it up to that reason and the conversation ended.

A few years later, I had the occasion to be in Las Vegas for a dental convention. I decided to see my former patient and make sure he still had his teeth. I always assume the treatment is successful. Otherwise, they would be in touch with me. But assumption is the mother of most misunderstanding. This was an opportunity to make this determination personally.

As soon as I arrived in Las Vegas, I telephoned my patient and we had a nice chat. As far as I could determine, he was not having problems with his teeth. He asked if I was busy the next evening and if I was interested in attending a private party being given for Joe DiMaggio. It seems people were always making parties for Joe. In light of what had happened previously I was leery, but my patient told me not to be concerned. He thought we might determine why he walked out of my office.

The party was held in a small, private room, where a trio of musicians was playing soft music. Joe was sitting alone at his table, in the center of the room, with a holier-than-thou look on his face as though he was a King holding court. His court hovered and congregated around him, poised to attend his every need. Someone was always available if Joe needed something. If Joe had a desire, all the arrangements would be made for him and the court would take care of any expense. After all, during his career, he was a King of baseball.

My patient escorted me to Joe and introduced me. He extended his hand, we shook, and there was a beaming smile on his face. When he was in my office, I never met him. We chatted for a while, the conversation being light and diverting, and then I asked if he recalled being in my New York office? A quizzical look came over his face, as though he was retrieving something amusing from the past. I reminded him that he walked out of the reception room without filling out my health questionnaire. I told him I was concerned that perhaps my receptionist had inadvertently insulted him or made him feel uncomfortable. If so, I would certainly like to know in order to remedy the situation and avoid it ever happening again.

"Oh, I remember that day," Joe replied, a smile crossing his face. "I thought the receptionist was trying to get my autograph and I didn't think that was appropriate so I walked out. Sorry."

I thought to myself, what a dingbat! I could not believe he thought we asked him to fill out a health questionnaire just for his autograph. In fact, there was no place on the questionnaire for a signature.

Sooooo . . . I met Joe DiMaggio, never treated him, and never got his autograph. More important, he never had the privilege of being treated by me.

GOOD JUDGEMENT COMES FROM EXPERIENCE AND A LOT OF THAT COMES FROM BAD JUDGEMENT.

WILL ROGERS

TWELVE

Another signature tale

A few years later, an incident similar to the one involving Joe DiMaggio occurred. A patient of mine, a very attractive young lady, asked if I would treat her boyfriend. "Of course," I replied happily. "A new patient provides me with the green paper to pay bills and allows me to maintain the lifestyle to which I am accustomed." Subsequently, she made an appointment for him for a cleaning and examination.

This new patient was punctual for his appointment. He entered the office and announced to the receptionist that he was "Gino." My receptionist, Carol, welcomed him with a warm smile and asked him to fill out the required health questionnaire. Thousands of prior patients had followed this routine procedure. He looked at the questionnaire, rolled his eyes and looked at Carol, gave her a broad smile, and politely said,

"No thanks."

Returning the questionnaire, he briskly walked out the door. Shades of Joe DiMaggio, it was déjà vu. This was not a celebrity worrying about his autograph. However, there appeared to be one commonality. They were both Italian. Was it something in their genes? What was going on?

I called Gino's girlfriend and recounted the incident. She did not seem surprised and asked for another appointment for him. She urged me not to request that he fill out any papers. I told her that I would see "Gino" and discuss the necessity of supplying needed information.

Again, Gino was on time and was escorted to my private office, a procedure prearranged with my receptionist. When I walked into my office, Gino was smoking a cigarette. Subsequently, much to my chagrin, I discovered that he was a heavy smoker, at least five packs of cigarettes a day. During our conversation, Gino appeared to be a nice guy, calm and friendly, but not excited about sitting in a dental chair. After being informed that certain fundamental information was needed or I would not do any dentistry for him, he agreed to tell me "all." However, he stipulated that nothing would be written down. I received ominous vibes. Was there something sinister underlying this conversation? I finally agreed to write down only what was absolutely necessary for future visits. Additionally, his file would be labeled with a fictitious name and would be kept locked in my private desk. Gino did not know that my desk did not have a lock. Despite the cloak and dagger routine, he was especially charming and likable.

Gino reached into his pocket, pulled out an envelope bulging with money and counted off ten mint one hundred dollar bills. He said his girlfriend thought I was the best dentist in New York City. Had she taken an accurate sampling of the dentists in the city? He wanted "top caliber work." In an imperious manner, he declared that money was no object. "Don't worry about the cost, Doc. Each week one of my associates will appear with 'green,' (his favorite word) even if I can't keep the appointment."

The examination revealed that Gino required extensive restorative dentistry, the result of years of neglect. When informed of the fee, which was significant, he declared "not to worry!" Those of us fortunate to be raised on the streets of New York understood the meaning of these words.

"Just do the best job Doc, use the best materials no matter how expensive, and each week expect your delivery."

True to his word, every week part of my fee was received in crisp one hundred dollar bills. One delivery was accompanied by his compliments and a large fish wrapped in dry ice. Fortunately, it was not a fish head so I did not take this to be symbolically threatening. Gino had a sense of humor.

Gino was treated for several months; suddenly, he stopped making appointments. Each week crisp, new one hundred dollar bills continued to arrive by messenger until the entire fee was paid. However, less than half his treatment was complete. At this point, Gino was wearing provisional restorations and further damage to his teeth could follow if he did not receive permanent restorations.

Gino could not be located. We contacted his girlfriend and this proved fruitless. Approximately six months later, Gino called the office indicating he was back and ready to resume treatment. During his six-month hiatus, considerable additional damage had occurred to his teeth. Gino had no issue with the additional fee requested.

"Just fix 'em up Doc," he said with a friendly smile.

After resuming treatment, Gino made an astonishing confession. "Doc," he said, "they had me in jail on a murder charge. Would you believe that? I don't do murder, Doc. I'm involved with women, gambling, and other things, but I don't do murder. They figured if they kept me in jail and put pressure on me I would 'rat' on who did the murder. They knew I didn't do the murder so finally they had to let me out."

What was suspected was finally confirmed; Gino had to be part of the Mafia. It was pure deduction. I was acting like Sherlock Holmes. Well, perhaps more like Dr. Watson. Slowly, Gino began to take me into his confidence. We had a good relationship and he confided in me. He told me that one Christmas, in his early married years, he did not have money to buy gifts for his kids. He went into his attic, got a gun, and held up several bookies and loan sharks in order to raise money to buy his kids presents. He covered his face with a ski mask so they could not recognize him. He said he would only hold up gamblers or loan sharks because they were ripping off innocent people. So why not steal from them? I wondered about his logic and his ethical code. During another conversation, he revealed the contract rate for various intimidating or retaliative injuries to others. The cost of breaking someone's leg was fifty thousand dollars. The price for breaking both legs, he added, would be the same because his costs would not change. He explained that a "fee" could be high if the victim had to be followed for several weeks to determine his pattern of behavior. In this manner, the "damages" could be delivered at the appropriate time without him being implicated in the crime. Time costs money. To him it was all business. Note his use of business terminology: contract, time, fees, price, costs, damages and delivered.

When he was in the office, Gino was always extremely kind and courteous to my staff. On occasions when my wife or daughter happened to be in the office, he was a gentleman, always inquiring of their health and wishing them well. His sense of respect made me feel as though I wanted to be his friend. I definitely did not want to be his enemy.

During the course of his treatment, he gave me his business card. The name "Gino" was printed prominently on the top without any last name. It listed his telephone number and "Bridgeport, Connecticut." There was no street address. Apparently, he was well known in certain circles. "Keep it in your wallet at all times, Doc," he said. "I'll be very upset if I find you were in my town and didn't call me." I put the card into my wallet. He was obviously very sincere. He respected me and that respect was returned.

After completing his treatment, he returned regularly for follow-up and maintenance appointments. Never knowing his address, my staff was unable to send him appointment reminders. I was tempted to address an appointment reminder card to him using only his first name. I wondered whether the Post Office would be able to deliver it? Gino made it his responsibility to remember when to make appointments. His phone number could always be found in my wallet. Perhaps it gave me a sense of security knowing someone would be there for me in Bridgeport should help ever be needed.

At one point, several years passed without hearing from him. I assumed he was once again in jail, but this was not confirmed by his girlfriend who returned regularly to my office. On one occasion, she told me she hadn't seen him for several years and they were no longer going together. This may have been true but I believe she knew where he was.

Gino had been in prison and after his release returned to my office for dental maintenance. Gino was treated by me for more than twenty-five years until his death from lung and brain cancer.

I NEVER LIE
UNLESS IT'S IMPORTANT.

THE AUTHOR

**FRIENDSHIP IS PRECIOUS, NOT ONLY IN
THE SHADE, BUT IN THE SUNSHINE
OF LIFE. AND THANKS TO A BENEVOLENT
ARRANGEMENT, THE GREATER PART
OF LIFE IS SUNSHINE.**

THOMAS JEFFERSON

THIRTEEN

The tale's end

One cloudless and windless summer day, I was sailing with
my family on Long Island Sound. The water was showered with
bright sunlight that reflected in a blinding dazzle, blanketing the
boat with oppressive heat. Not a ripple disturbed the water. Sailors
often characterize calm as the simultaneous disappearance of
the wind and the appearance of a cold beer. Such was not the
case. We were in an alcohol-free dead calm!

My wife and children complained bitterly about the heat and
begged me to start the engine. They believed the forward motion
of the boat would generate an artificial breeze and produce a
cooling effect. They were right! However, we were in a sailboat,
not a motor boat. Being a classical sailor, I believe a boat's
movement should depend on the wind. Otherwise, I would have
been on a motor boat with the comforts of air conditioning
and the ability to go anywhere I desired. I recalled the maxim,

"The Captain is always right." Misinformed perhaps, sloppy, crude, bull headed, fickle, often stubborn, even stupid, but never wrong.

This adventure or perhaps misadventure had its beginning two months earlier when my wife suggested that my oldest son Sidney and I take sailing lessons. She thought it was a wonderful way for us to bond. Furthermore, she knew I was intrigued by thoughts of sailing. Books and movies about tall ships and square riggers fascinated me. I often dreamed of commanding such ships, the wind blowing across my receding hairline as the violent elements were battled and the vessel successfully plowed through torrential seas.

One of my patients, Mr. Miles Jackson, owned the Huntington Bay School of Sailing, located close to my home in Farmingdale, New York. One day, I approached him and offered to barter the dentistry he needed for sailing lessons. He was amenable to the suggestion and a deal was struck. My life as a sailor had begun. Every weekend during the months of June and July, my son and I drove to Huntington Bay to take lessons. Our training began on a fourteen-foot boat. Instruction covered a variety of topics: the intricacies of steering; sail management; effects of the wind on sails; positioning of the sails to maximize the wind's power; boat handling; response of boats under normal conditions; docking at a mooring; and the methods of securing a boat to a dock. Each lesson lasted 3-4 hours depending upon the amount of information presented and weather conditions. Our training was hands-on and conducted on the water. If it rained, we worked indoors on the theory of sailing and navigation. After our fourth weekend, we were promoted to a thirty-two-foot sloop which had a mainsail and a jib or headsail. This larger boat required greater responsibility because of its value and size. Fortunately, this boat turned and responded more slowly than the fourteen-foot boat, so there was more time to react to situations and make appropriate decisions.

After six weekends of instruction, Miles commented that I had a natural nautical ability. He noted my mastery of basic sailing techniques and my need to practice more in order to become an accomplished sailor. For the next few weeks, sailing the boat with Miles aboard, I acted as the Captain making all the nautical decisions. Miles would offer suggestions if he felt that trouble might develop. Fortunately, this never happened. Each time after docking, he would critique my performance. One day, he jumped on my butt for making a terrible dock approach. Another time, he chewed me out for improperly setting the sails. That was two times I was imperfect. My ego was slowly being crushed.

In the beginning of August, Miles felt lessons were no longer necessary. He suggested we use one of his boats and continue our sailing, perhaps staying overnight at an anchorage in Connecticut and returning the next day. Thoughtfully, he volunteered to help work out the arrangements.

We checked the nautical charts, selected Strathmore, Connecticut as the anchorage site and began making a list of supplies needed for our two-day sail. A thirty-foot sailboat was selected from Miles' fleet, a sloop that slept four, two in the main cabin and two in the "V" berth. The term "V" meant there was one bunk on the port side and one on the starboard side of the bow and joined together they formed a "V." A berth or bunk on a boat describes any horizontal surface whose total area does not exceed one-half of the surface of an average person at rest.

My wife and daughter decided to accompany us on the trip. I was the captain, my son Sid the first mate, my daughter Lois ordinary seaman, though she was far from ordinary, and my wife, Bella, the best mate. At the time, my son was fourteen and my daughter twelve. It is inappropriate to discuss my wife's age because of the threat of her increasing my vertical challenge. I cannot afford to be any shorter!

The morning of our departure, we packed the car with

supplies, drove to Huntington Bay and loaded the boat. The sailboat was already equipped with the essentials for sailing, such as life jackets and a marine radio.

At 10:00 a.m., we slipped away from the dock under motor. Once outside the bay, we hoisted the sails and turned off the engine. We sailed for the first time under my command. No one on board had more sailing knowledge than me. I was, in truth, the main man, the Captain, the figurehead frequently described as the decorative dummy found on sailboats. I tried not to show my nervousness but my stammered commands must have been obvious. A soft breeze caused the sails to curve out tautly and everyone enjoyed the moment. The charm of sailing includes the movement and immensity of the water, the vastness of the sky, the clear air, the wind and salt spray blowing on graying hair, and the tuneful sough of the wind passing over the sails.

We moved at a slow but steady pace, making approximately three knots. A knot is a unit of speed of one nautical mile (6075 feet) an hour. About noon, my wife went below to the galley to prepare sandwiches and drinks for the Captain and crew. The galley represents an aspect of seafaring associated with slavery - both ancient and modern. A "galley slave" was a person condemned to row the galleys of the ancient world. In modern times, it is the person relegated (condemned) to the boat's kitchen, the galley, and who is responsible for providing food and beer to the Captain and who also provides an aspect of seafaring associated with slavery.

We discovered that Bella never became seasick. She was the only person in our family capable of going below during foul weather. If the other crew members went below, especially in rough seas, they invariably became incapacitated because of "mal de mer" or seasickness. Bella, our "slave," was given complete charge of the galley in recognition of her sea hardiness. I don't think she appreciated the honor, but understood the difficulties the rest of us had and went along like a good sport.

At about two o'clock the wind died. I was previously advised this often occurred in the afternoon. It could last until 5-6 p.m. when the evening breezes arrived. It was now 4:00 p.m. and we had been sitting motionlessly roasting in the heat. I had difficulty convincing my crew that seasoned sailors rely upon the whim of the wind for vessel movement. I hinted that putting on the motor would be tantamount to accepting defeat.

But convincing my skeptical crew was increasingly difficult. About 5:00 p.m. my wife, in a concerned voice, remarked that it was beginning to get dark. I looked up. Cloud patterns were forming and swallowing the sun. In the east, a dark shroud of clouds loomed over the water. Darkness was pushing the light out of the sky. It was becoming dark too early for this time of year. I could see thunder heads in the distance and realized a storm was brewing. In the late afternoon during this part of the summer, squalls frequently appear suddenly and unexpectedly on Long Island Sound causing chaos among boaters. To relieve my crew's anxiety, I remarked casually that the engine would be started. It was getting darker and I was becoming more concerned. When I turned the ignition key to start the engine, my son began lowering the jib and mainsail. The starter turned over but the engine did not. I tried again with the same result. As the sky darkened, a crisp breeze sprang up. Again, I turned the key, the starter turned over and roared into life but the engine did not start. Perhaps the engine was flooded? I decided to wait a few minutes before trying again. Now, the sky was pitch black; the wind began to howl fiercely and seemed to strengthen with each passing minute. The black line of clouds that appeared in the east was rolling in with a fury. The rippling water turned into mounting waves. Rain came down in thick sheets. Bolts of lightening illuminated the sky followed by continuous thunderclaps.

The engine was tried again but it was futile. Remaining calm, I asked my son to raise the jib and mainsail. Wind power would allow us to escape the approaching storm. Regarding me curiously, he did not understand why we were raising the sails after having just lowered them. Realization struck him: we were in the middle of a storm. With my daughter's assistance, he raised the mainsail and the jib. Though Lois had not taken any sailing lessons, she quickly learned how to work the sails.

Although I read a great deal about boat handling in a storm and understood its complexities, I never captained a boat in these conditions and I was becoming increasingly alarmed. Initially, I was overwhelmed by uncertainty. Then my nautical instincts kicked in. After resetting the sails and explaining the situation to my crew, I asked my son to tend the tiller while I went below to look at the nautical charts. The tiller is a horizontal bar connected to the rudder, a flat plate at the back of the boat which when turned causes the vessel to change direction. We were caught in a storm without a working engine and therefore had to depend solely on the wind for movement.

The increased wind velocity caused the boat to move at about six knots. However, I was unsure if we were going in a safe direction. While trying to remain calm and to think positively, it was apparent that I needed to determine our present location and the nearest safe haven.

It was about 6:00 p.m. The wind velocity increased to more than twenty knots with stronger gusts. Thunderclaps growled ominously with fierce and frequent lightening strikes. Stinging pellets of rain came in blinding sheets. Waves smashed against the boat and the Sound was increasingly choppy. Earlier, we had passed a marker buoy so I knew our approximate location. But this was insufficient. We had to know our exact location in order to plot a safe course. Fortunately, we passed another marker buoy. Now the boat's position could be accurately established. According to the nautical chart, we were approximately six miles southwest of the harbor entrance to Bridgeport, Connecticut.

This was the closest and safest haven. I immediately set

a course for this destination. Ideally, sailing northeast at our present speed would take us about one hour to arrive at the harbor's entrance. But the wind was blowing from the northeast and a sailboat cannot sail directly into the wind. The boat must "tack" to allow the wind to blow over the port or starboard quarter of the boat's bow, resulting in forward movement. To tack, the bow must pass through the direction the wind is blowing from so the wind can pass from one side of the boat to the other. During the tacking maneuver, the wind momentarily blows directly against the front of the sails, tending to stop the boat. If the boat is not traveling fast enough while passing through the force of the direct wind, or if the sails are not hauled to the opposite side of the boat at the right moment, the boat could be stopped completely or even blown backward. At the very least, it would severely hamper the boat's forward movement.

To reach our destination would require several tacks causing the boat to go toward Bridgeport indirectly. Each tack results in a zigzag course as the boat moves upwind. This zigzagging considerably increases the amount of time needed to reach our destination. It was now past 6:00 p.m. The rain continued to fall and the winds blew steadily. The blackened sky severely limited visibility.

When the rain began, my son and I put on foul weather gear: weather proof coveralls and jacket, and a large weather proof hat. Our weather proof rubber boots helped keep us warm and dry and offered increased security on the slippery, shifting wet deck. Foul weather gear, in nautical terms, is defined as weatherproof clothing usually needed in spring, summer, fall, and winter. Unfortunately, we did not take weather proof gloves. They would have been welcome in the cold rain. Over this gear, we put on life jackets.

Following a zigzag course with repeated tacks, we beat into the wind on a course as near to the direction of the wind as possible. Sailboats are designed to lie over on their side or heel when sailing close to the wind. Heeling begins with the boat leaning over as the wind presses on one side of the sails. The boat heeled sharply. When a sailboat cannot handle wind pressure, usually something gives, a deck fitting pulls out, a sail rips, or a mast snaps. The boat will stay upright if it has a keel with suitable ballast (heavy material placed low in a vessel to improve its stability). Fortunately, our boat had suitable ballast. To prevent the possibility of a mishap, we put a single reef in the mainsail. A reef shortens the sail, reducing the sail's surface area exposed to the increasingly strong wind. This lessens the wind's influence on the sail, effectively decreasing the heel of the boat. However, it reduced the speed of our boat. Even with this safety measure to reduce the heeling, the deck was inundated with water caused by the waves breaking over the boat. Everybody was soaked. We battened down all the hatches to prevent water from accumulating below the deck.

To alert the crew, I hollered loudly above the roar of the storm and gave the crew sufficient time to prepare before each tack.

"Ready to come about."

I then shouted, "Helm's alee," indicating the tiller would be pushed away from the wind causing the boat to change direction and "come about." My son released the jib sheet, the line that held down the clew or bottom corner of the sail. The jib passed to the other side of the boat along with the mainsail, which is self-tending. The boom is attached to a device called a "traveler," which allows the sail to move unattended to the port or starboard of the boat.

The bow of the boat moved through the direction the wind was coming from. After the boat passed through this imaginary line, the position of the tiller was centered while my son tied down the jib sheet. After completing the tack, the boat moved from a northerly to an easterly direction. Following several tacks and zigzagging through the eye of the wind, we arrived at the mouth of Bridgeport Harbor. Specks of light against a vast black background were the only visible items in the storm-filled night. Now, it was past 10:00 p.m.

Bridgeport's harbor is long and narrow with its marina, or commercial dock facility, located at the innermost part. Unfortunately, the wind was blowing directly out of the harbor. The thunderstorm had finally passed, but the sky was still dark and the water rough. The harbor's narrowness caused us to make repeated short tacks to reach the inner harbor. The Bridgeport ferry, which frequently enters and leaves the harbor, created a problem. Our tacks were carefully timed to avoid any collision. I decided to tack behind the ferry to avert this possibility. This made the control of our boat difficult because we had to traverse the wake of the ferry. Darkness and rain made the maneuvers difficult and exhausting. Crossing the ferry's wake caused the bow of our boat to dip below water. To avoid this, I tried to cross the wake diagonally. However, this caused the boat to bob and roll so everyone had to hold firmly onto the boat to avoid injury. This frightened my crew and caused me great anxiety. As we traveled farther into the harbor, the wind velocity decreased. To manage a sailboat, sufficient wind power is essential. Otherwise, the boat will lose steerage making control more difficult. The ferries kept coming in and out of the harbor and we kept tacking. It was strenuous work. I was fortunate to have my son and daughter to handle the sails. At about 11:30 p.m., we caught the first glimpse of the harbor's inner docks.

Suddenly, I was aware that without a working engine, the boat would have to be docked under sail. Moorings were not visible. Docking a boat under sail without the use of an engine is an extremely difficult maneuver under ideal conditions. A boat has no brakes, but is slowed by drag created by its movement through the water. If the current is moving opposite to the boat's direction, this helps slow the boat down. However, if the boat is moving in the same direction as the current, the boat's forward speed will be increased. A current coming from the port or starboard may help or hinder the docking process. The direction of the current or whether there was a slack tide (no current at all) was unknown. I had to visually gauge the boat's distance from the dock, know the speed of the boat, factor in any windage and tidal forces, and then drop the sails at the precise moment to allow the boat to gently glide through the water until it touched the dock. If the sails are dropped too soon, there may be insufficient forward movement to reach the dock. The boat, driven by wind and current, may drift off in an unwanted direction. Dropping the sails too late may cause the boat to be driven into the dock by these same forces. This could result in damage to the boat, dock, or both depending on the vessel's velocity. Fortunately, the strong winds and heavy rains had abated. But it was still pitch black and the poor visibility made it difficult to judge distances.

What a dilemma! I had never docked a boat under sail. It is not a situation that is practiced at sailing school. Bella was told to sit down and hold tight. Sid and Lois were advised of the problem and each was asked to handle one sail and when I hollered, "down sails," to do it rapidly. I explained these procedures as if they were routine in order to avoid anxiety in my crew.

"Just bring them down as quickly as you can," I said.

The appropriate time to drop the sails was a guess. We moved closer to the dock and I hollered,

"Down sails!"

My kids got them down fast enough while I prayed that I had selected the appropriate moment. With the sails down, we were at the mercy of wind, current, and boat speed. The boat glided toward the dock. It seemed to take forever. Anticipating a crash, I hollered "Hold on."

You could feel the boat decelerate. Would it slow down sufficiently? Finally, the boat drifted to the dock without a bump. It was a perfect docking procedure under sail. My first and it was pure luck.

Sid and I quickly jumped onto the dock and tied the boat to the pier. We placed soft plastic devices called fenders on the side of the boat, fore and aft. These are used to protect the boat from rubbing against the dock. We were on land and for the moment safe, or was this an illusion?

Visibility was poor due to the darkness and thick mist. Several boats were tied to other docks. In the distance, there was a flight of stairs to the street level. They were illuminated poorly by a street lamp. The shrouding mist made the entire area eerie and scary. There were two options, neither one good: stay with the boat or walk up the stairs. We had plenty of food and water, therefore, staying aboard was a viable option. The second option, moving to the street, seemed the least desirable. Once on the street, we would encounter the same problems. We would not know our location or where to go. Furthermore, we would be exposed to the cold, wet, misty night.

While removing our foul weather gear, suddenly someone shouted from the street.

"Hello there, are you guys all right?"

Though his voice startled us, the sound was welcomed.

"We're OK," I responded, and gave the "voice" a quick review of our entire day.

"Well, I wouldn't linger here too long. Someone was murdered here last week. It's not a safe area!" Then the figure vanished into the mist.

We had to find a safe place. My family was anxious and fearful. Suddenly, an idea popped into my head. I hurried to the boat, located my wallet, and removed Gino's business card. This was his town; hopefully, he would be able to help us.

Turning on the boat's Marine radio, I contacted the operator and gave her Gino's telephone number. The phone rang several times. Finally, someone at the other end picked up the phone and said,

"Yeah."

"Go ahead with your call please," the marine operator said, and I quickly asked,

"Is Gino there?"

"Who's dis?" replied the person. There was a great deal of noise and music in the background.

"I'm Dr. Jones, Gino's dentist. Gino once told me . . ."

"Holy Cow," screamed the voice at the other end. "I'm Gino's brudda, Frankie. He tol' me if youz ever called to take care of ya. Where the heck is ya?"

I told him our approximate location.

"Don't youz move. Look for a white limo."

Before he hung up, I heard him screaming at someone named Sal to get down to the docks.

It seemed like an eternity, but probably no more than fifteen minutes passed when a white stretch limousine, the longest stretch limo I had ever seen, stopped next to the stairway. The door opened and a short, stocky man appeared out of the mist. His footfall on the creaky stairs disturbed the silent night.

"Hi," he shouted. "I'm Sal, is youz guys good?"

Sal was a short, very stocky man wearing a sport jacket and no tie. He was square jawed with a short stubble on his face. He appeared to be a very powerful man. There was a bulge under his jacket's handkerchief pocket, which made him appear even more sinister.

"Yea," I replied, "we're fine!"

"Gino's brudda, Frankie, said I should come pick youz guys up and take youz to his joint. So, get any things ya needs and let's get going. Dis place is bad." He did not appear to be a person who scared easily.

I quickly locked up the boat while the others proceeded to

the street. We jumped into the limo and found it had a full bar and reclining seats. It felt more like a recreational vehicle than a limousine. Sal got behind the wheel and off we sped.

I opened the window to get an idea of the area. It was still very misty with poor visibility. The houses, typical of a run-down waterfront, were mostly wood-frame, in disrepair, and many were boarded up and gloomy. The architecture seemed early twentieth century.

As we continued, the appearance of the houses and neighborhoods improved. Many were constructed of brick, well kept and landscaped, typical of a middle to an upper-middle class area. Farther on, the houses reverted to poor, shabby, and dilapidated.

We made a turn and suddenly the streets became a waste land. It looked like London or Berlin after the devastation of World War II. The area was rubble with an occasional wall still standing. We continued through this depressing area for a few more blocks and suddenly a single, intact building stood in the midst of the ruins.

The car stopped in front of this red brick building and Sal got out. Smoke seeped through the doors. I thought the structure was on fire. With all the surrounding debris, I wondered if they could find a fire hydrant? Perhaps they would use a male dog? Then I heard music. Sal, sensing my astonishment said,

"Here we is! Dis is Gino's night club. Let's go in and find his brudda, Frankie."

When we entered, smoke poured out of the building. I resisted the urge to scream "Fire!" The sound of music roared through the smoke-filled, open doorway. The noise from the band and the nightclub's patrons was deafening. It was Saturday night, but this had to be the granddaddy of all parties. People of both sexes and all ages were packed wall to wall, some sitting, some standing, and some dancing on a wooden floor. Nearly everyone was smoking a cigarette, the obvious cause of the smoke.

Sal asked us to wait and walked away. A few moments later, he came out of a back room with someone that looked like Gino's twin. For a split second, I thought it was Gino.

"Hey, Doc, how ya doin'," he said. "I'm Gino's brudda, Frankie."

With that declaration, he grasped my hand, shook it, then grabbed me and kissed me on both cheeks. I knew this was a European or Italian thing, but a glance from my son told me he thought Gino's brother was gay. I introduced my family. Frankie did not make any attempt to kiss my wife or daughter. When he extended his hand, my son stepped back to avoid being hugged and kissed.

Frankie explained that Gino was in Brooklyn and had told him years ago that if his dentist ever called when he wasn't around to make sure to take care of him.

"So anything youz needs, youz got," Frankie said. "Have youz guys eaten?"

It was now after two o'clock in the morning, not our usual dinner time. However, from the day's stress and hard work we were famished. I told my new buddy Frankie that we didn't want to put him out.

"Don' worry. I'll take care of it." He called Sal and commanded, "Tell the chef to put up some steaks, shrimp, and lobster for deez guys, pronto." Sal quickly took off toward the kitchen.

Frankie looked around the club; I could visualize the light bulb go on. Frankie was obviously thinking about where we could sit. At every table designed for eight people there were ten sitting and another four or five standing. I had no idea where the people dancing belonged. Perhaps, at a particular moment, a certain number of patrons sitting or standing would move to dance and the previous dancers would have seats.

Frankie continued looking around. Suddenly, he pointed to a table adjacent to the dance floor. He waved his hand and shouted,

"Hey, . . . youz, . . . move!"

The people at the table turned around, looked at Frankie, froze for a moment and then, in unison, quietly disappeared into the crowd. It was a Moses-like miracle, with Frankie parting the patrons.

Suddenly, there was an empty table in the midst of a sea of human beings. The four of us were seated at a table designed to accommodate eight. Frankie appointed Sal our personal valet. He came and sat with us. Whatever we needed, all we had to do was ask.

Soon, steaks, shrimp, lobster, and veggies arrived at our table family style. We ate voraciously. You tend to lose your appetite when you are anxious, but it certainly returns with a vengeance when the fear abates. Bella and I had a couple of drinks while eating and the kids had sodas. The late hour made it feel more like breakfast. Sal continually inquired if I needed tires for my car. He would "order" four terrific Michelin tires and, since the boss was my friend, he would give me a great deal. With that lump under his jacket, I was concerned whether it was wise to say no. Sal was hard to read. You never saw a thing on the surface, no matter how long you studied his face. In all fairness, there never was a moment that we did not feel absolutely safe and welcomed. The situation was bizarre, but the sense of safety was always present.

It was 5:00 a.m. I told Frankie it was time for us to return to the boat. He was concerned for our safety, but I assured him that it would soon be light and we would be OK.

"Is dare anything youz guys needs?" Frankie asked.

I requested some ice for the boat.

"No sweat. Hey, Sal, get Doc some ice for da boat."

Sal hurried off to the kitchen and moments later returned with a large cake of ice. It had to be at least forty pounds; it was melting all over Sal's sport jacket.

"No, no," I said. "That's too much ice. About a quarter of that amount would be great. It has to fit in a small ice chest on board the boat."

Sal went back to the kitchen and reappeared with the right size ice. This time the ice was housed in a cardboard box and Sal put it in the limo's trunk. We thanked Frankie and his friends for their wonderful hospitality. Kiddingly, I told Frankie he better not forget to tell Gino about my visit or I'd have to bust up his nose, but not his teeth, otherwise I would have to fix them. He laughed. It was good he could take a joke.

We did not get back to the boat until six a.m. We made the boat shipshape, ready to get under way for our return to Huntington Bay.

To my crew, I invoked an old Irish toast, "May the winds always be at our back." This is a sailor's wish that winds should come from behind the boat since these are the most favorable. A quick look at the telltales indicated the wind was blowing in the best direction, at least for the present. Telltales are small pieces of cloth or string which are attached to some part of the rigging of the boat and serve to indicate the direction of the wind. If we were lucky, this wind would hold and take us directly to Huntington Bay without the necessity of tacking or using any other maneuver.

The lines tying the boat to the dock were released and we pulled in the fenders. The tiller was put in a neutral position while Sid raised the mainsail. As the wind filled the sail, the boat moved smartly away from the dock and into the harbor channel. Sid set the jib and the boat moved briskly. With the sails finally in their proper setting, we did almost four knots, a nice pace. This wind would take us directly out of the harbor and into Long Island Sound.

In the Sound, the wind maintained its direction so I pointed the boat toward Huntington Bay. It was a beautiful day which often follows after a storm. In the middle of the Sound, the wind died down slightly, but we maintained a speed of three knots. In the early afternoon, we arrived at the entrance to Huntington Bay.

Throughout the entire trip across the Sound, I thought about our failed engine. To enter a crowded harbor under sail was sheer madness. During the storm there was no choice and my success was pure luck. Prudently, I decided to hail a power boat near the harbor's entrance and request a tow. Boaters tend to stick together, even though there is a rivalry between stink-potters (power-boaters) and sail-boaters. It would give the power boat owner temporary bragging rights that a motor boat can go anywhere at any time but a sailboat cannot.

At the appropriate moment, a suitable power boat was flagged down and I explained our situation to Bob, the captain. He was very accommodating and agreed to tow us into Huntington Bay. He ran a heavy line through the chocks, hornlike metal projections curved inward and attached to the boat, and then the line was tied to a cleat on each boat. In a short time, the boat was moored.

I noticed that Bob's chock appeared to be damaged and offered to buy him a new one. He did not know its cost but agreed to inform me later. We exchanged contact information and discovered that we worked in the same building in New York City. The following week, Bob called with the chock's cost, and I gladly paid. Bob became one of my patients and I treated him for many years.

A few years later, I was in a financial position to buy my own sailboat. It was known as a Friendship sloop because it was originally designed and built in Friendship, Maine. (See Chapter 14).

One summer, while sailing on Vineyard Sound traveling from Vineyard Haven to Newport, Rhode Island we were struck by a major storm and had to take refuge in Cuttyhunk, Massachusetts. Though our engine did not fail this time, our experience in the Bridgeport storm was invaluable to our survival. But that's a story for another time.

THE GREATEST LESSON IN LIFE IS TO KNOW THAT EVEN FOOLS ARE RIGHT SOMETIMES.

SIR WINSTON CHURCHILL

ONLY THE GUY WHO ISN'T ROWING HAS TIME TO ROCK THE BOAT.

JEAN-PAUL SARTRE

FOURTEEN

The Boat

Exactly when my love of sailboats and the sea first began is lost in the mist of time. But it began at an early age. I vividly recall being mesmerized while watching sailboats glide across a lake or slice through the ocean's waves. Sailing is an exciting experience. Dreams of owning a sailboat are the next best thing. Now a senior citizen, watching boats under sail still remains an exhilarating experience.

In 1974, at the age of forty-one, I had a heart attack. I spent three weeks in a hospital followed by three more weeks recuperating at home. Many friends visited me during this period and one in particular, Andy, who played a special part in this story. He was older than me, extremely wealthy, and owned a small, beautiful Norwegian day-sailer. He knew of my love for sailing and occasionally asked me to go with him on a day sail. Those were wondrous days and I savored them.

During Andy's visits, we chatted about many things. He mentioned that he was no longer enamored with his day-sailer and he was looking to buy a bigger boat, one that would make sailing easier for his wife. Not an enthusiastic sailor, she wanted a more comfortable setting, readily available on larger vessels. While describing a sloop he recently inspected, my heart pounded with envy. Bella, my wife, a keenly observant person, noticed my excitement and suggested that Andy take me to see the boat he contemplated buying. Andy agreed. Under my breath I let out a substantial "Whoopee."

The following week we went to see the boat at the Huntington Harbor docks. Upon seeing the sailboat, my heart began to race. For a moment, I thought "another heart attack." The human body's reaction to excitement is amazing.

Except in movies, I had never seen a sailboat like this nor been aboard one like it. Andy explained that the boat was a replica of a Friendship Sloop, so called because they were originally built in the town of Friendship, Maine. The boat was thirty feet long on deck and had a ten-foot bowsprit, making the overall length forty feet. It had five sails; a mainsail, staysail, jib, main topsail and jib topsail. I later discovered its spruce mast had no knots and was forty-seven feet tall, measured from the water line to its top. It had to have been fashioned from a tree with an enormous circumference to result in a suitable mast size without knots. The boat slept four, had a head (bathroom), a heated cabin, and an onboard freezer. The hull was fiberglass, the deck teak, and all other features were exact duplicates of those found on Friendship sloops built before the turn of the twentieth century. These boats were designed for lobster fishing before the advent of marine engines. It had a very long keel, a ten-foot beam, a wide bottom, and low gunnels (the upper edge of the sides of the boat). When the sails were set and the steering wheel placed in a fixed position, the boat would sail in a straight line. Because of this feature and its low gunnels, a fisherman could drop and retrieve his lobster traps without assistance.

Modern sailboats rely on winches for the power to raise sails. This boat, designed before the advent of winches, used Lignum Vitae (extremely hard, fossilized wood) blocks and tackle as the sail raising power system in the tradition of old sailing vessels. With all sails unfurled, it resembled a boat the actor Errol Flynn used in one of his sea sagas.

When Andy asked my opinion, I became exuberant, almost to the point of embarrassment.

"Are you kidding?" I responded, excitedly. "It would be crazy NOT to buy the boat. It's special, different, and beautiful." I explained that he would be obtaining the best of two worlds, a boat with a fiberglass hull, easy and inexpensive to maintain, not that money was an issue, and a touch of history. His wife might even be pleased with the cabin's heater and freezer. In my excitement, I would have bought the boat . . . if it were not beyond my financial resources.

Andy purchased the boat and owned it for a couple of years. I had the distinct pleasure of sailing with him several times. However, there was a problem. The Friendship sloop, designed as a pleasure boat, needed one person tending the wheel and another to raise and lower the sails. Andy's wife, though a lovely person and a good sport, constantly rebelled about performing these tasks. Andy tried his wife at the wheel while he tended the sails but it did not work. The boat has to be pointing windward to reduce wind pressure to facilitate the raising and lowering of the sails. Andy's wife had a directionality problem, so maintaining the proper boat position was difficult for her. This made working the sails troublesome and Andy was not a youngster. On several occasions, he remarked that he would have gladly traded his wench for a winch.

Though Andy had a passion for cruising, he lacked an enthusiastic and reliable nautical mate. Andy and his wife tried several voyages with mixed results. Though the overall sailing experience was great, his wife was still unhappy. What a wonderful way to get rid of your wife. But, this was a longstanding, happy marriage. Andy did not want to jeopardize the relationship so he decided to sell the boat rather than face a divorce and its potential financial consequences.

Realizing how much I loved the boat, he called and asked me if I wanted to buy it. By now, my health was OK and handling the boat would not be a problem. Further, Bella had proven herself a great first mate, both as a spouse and nautical companion. Additionally, I had five children, one girl and four boys who could serve as crew. My problem was financial. My daughter was attending college and my two youngest sons would soon attend a private specialty school. The tuition for the three was considerable. I was unsure about my ability to purchase the boat and pay the tuition. Furthermore, maintaining such a boat was quite expensive.

Andy was disappointed. He would have loved for me to own the boat, since we could have sailed on it together. He also loved this unique boat. Finally, he decided to donate the boat to the Bath Maritime Museum in Bath, Maine and acquire a large tax deduction. The museum maintained the sloop in pristine condition and used it to demonstrate lobster fishing in the late nineteenth century.

Three years passed and the museum put the sloop up for sale in order to raise funds. Over the years, Andy had maintained contact with the director who called him and asked if he knew anyone who might be interested in purchasing the boat. In the interim, Andy had purchased a larger, more modern boat to make his wife's nautical life more enjoyable. Andy immediately thought of me and asked if I was interested in purchasing the boat.

Financially, my circumstances had changed. My dental practice was doing quite well. At this time, I could afford to buy and maintain the boat. After discussing this with Bella, we agreed to the purchase. Negotiations with the museum director commenced and the terms of the sale were finalized. The Coast Guard's requirements, including life jackets, the condition of the head and holding tank for waste were incorporated into the sale price. In hindsight, I wondered why "sale boats" cost so much? After purchasing the boat, I applied for membership to the Northport Yacht Club on Long Island Sound. It was accepted and the boat was delivered there.

However, there was one problem. Andy had registered the boat with the Coast Guard naming the boat "Betty," honoring his wife. This presented two options, keep the name of the boat "Betty" or change the name in which case the boat would have to be re registered with the Coast Guard. The first option was not acceptable. Furthermore, Bella and I believed a boat should never have a female name. We thought it sounded obscene every time someone said, "OK, let's everyone climb aboard 'Betty'." So we began an exhaustive search for a new name. "Sale Aboard," "Sea Nyle," "Nauti-Cal," and "Crew-Sing," were among the many names considered. None struck our fancy; they were too cute for a classical sailing vessel.

Several months passed. One day, while driving on the Long Island Expressway Bella suddenly and excitedly shouted,

"I've got it! I have got it! What a fantastic name for the boat. It's great! . . . It's perfect!"

"Sure, sure," I responded in an unencouraging tone. "It'll be just like all the other names."

"No, No," she exclaimed, with exhilaration in her voice. "This is for real. Listen! . . . Listen! . . . Let's name the boat 'Baschert'." [/ba'shert/]

When I heard the proposed name for the boat, I nearly drove off the roadway. "Baschert" is a Yiddish word that means "meant to be." It is frequently used in the pejorative sense, "nisht baschert," not meant to be. For example, a fellow and his girlfriend live together for five years and then decide to get married. They do so and six months later they get a divorce. Jewish commentary would suggest that the relationship was "nisht baschert." In our case, how fitting for the positive connotation of the word. We could not buy the boat the first time it was offered but received another chance. It was truly "Baschert." We were excited and immediately filed for a change of the boat's name with the Coast Guard. Upon approval, the name "Baschert" was painted on the transom.

We did not realize it at the moment, but the boat and its new name created unintended consequences. "Baschert" was so beautiful, especially when all five sails were unfurled, that million dollar cabin cruisers and motor launches would slow down to take pictures of us. This caused some anxious moments while underway. Even with the sails furled, pulling into a harbor would cause people to stop and stare at the boat. Frequently, people would shout across the water and ask if the pronunciation of the name of the boat was "Bear sh-t." Not very complimentary but we just shrugged it off.

Every summer for seven years, we plied the waters of Long Island Sound, Newport, and Block Island sailing as far as Martha's Vineyard and Nantucket. Our trips extended for two to three weeks depending on the amount of time I could take from my dental practice. As predicted, Bella turned out to be a great mate. I recognized this from her efforts on board the boat as well as the wonders she brought to our marriage. Additionally, the kids turned out to be a splendid crew. Though the boat only had four bunks, we often cruised with five or six people. The extra crew would sleep on deck or on the cabin sole. Frequently, one or more of the kids had prior commitments, so the entire family was rarely on board at the same time. On a day sail, the presence of the entire family was never a problem. As time passed and the kids got older and discovered there was an opposite sex, they were often AWOL from a sailing trip. But, I could always count on my faithful mate.

However, there came a time when Bella became ill and was unable to go sailing. Her condition prevented her from enjoying the time on the water. Without at least one crew member, I could not sail the boat. Frequently, with only a six-pack of beer as company, I would go down to the sloop lying at anchor, sit on deck and watch other boats enter and leave the harbor. It made me very sad. I decided to give up the boat. Though the decision was difficult, my dream had been fulfilled.

IT IS ILLEGAL
TO MAKE LIQUOR PRIVATELY
OR WATER PUBLICALLY.

LORD BIRKETT

OFTEN DESCRIBED AS THE BEST
CAPTAIN IN THE WORLD, I AM
FREQUENTLY ASKED IF THIS
IS TRUE? INVARIABLY, I RESPOND
THAT I MAY NOT BE THE BEST -
BUT THERE ARE NONE BETTER.

THE AUTHOR

FIFTEEN

The conclusion

After deciding to give up the boat, for-sale notices were placed in several newspapers and nautical magazines with the original cost of $38,000 the asking price. Although the boat was older, many expensive additions were made and I felt this amount was fair. There were several prospective buyers but no offers. Though they all agreed about its beauty and pristine condition, they were wary of the lack of winches on the boat. These are small revolving drums around which a rope or line is wound in order to increase the mechanical advantage thereby making it easier to pull the lines that control the sails.

I wanted to avoid costly winter storage charges and time was running short. My wife and I decided to donate "Baschert" to a charitable organization as defined in the Internal Revenue Service (IRS) code. Landmark, the specialty school my kids attended, had a sailing program and was such a charitable institution. We felt inclined to offer them the boat because they had done so much to help our children surmount their learning difficulties. We imposed one condition on our donation; specifically, the name "Baschert" could not be changed as long as they maintained ownership. The school was willing to accept the contribution with this stipulation.

To satisfy the IRS, we needed a letter of receipt from the institution and estimates from two marine appraisers testifying to the boat's value. If the appraisals were not comparable, a third would be required with the two closest estimates averaged and this sum used as the deduction. Two independent marine appraisers submitted valuations of $39,000 and $41,000 so $40,000 was used for tax purposes. My accountant advised us that there would be an automatic review of our tax return because of such a large deduction. He suggested we not worry; the contribution was legitimate and a reexamination was standard practice for a donation of this size.

Subsequently, we were informed by the IRS that after a thorough review of our tax return only an $8,000 deduction would be allowed. Therefore, $14,000 was owed in back taxes, penalties and interest. We were dumbfounded! My accountant remarked that he was licensed to practice before the IRS and, if necessary, would undertake our appeal. He felt strongly that the deduction was honest and proper. However, he did add that it was important to avoid the vagaries of the appeals court.

The IRS' valuation, my accountant learned, was predicated on a combination of two factors: the date the boat was built and the original price. In his opinion, this was an arbitrary and capricious appraisal. This determination was based on the IRS' nautical Blue Book. Unlike the Blue Book for cars, which has increased worth for special features such as air conditioning or spoked wheels, the nautical Blue Book did not allow for any additional values. We felt its pristine condition, the many expensive upgrades, and the legitimate appraisals by the two marine experts were not considered by the IRS in its evaluation. We arranged to meet with an IRS agent to appeal the judgement.

A few years earlier, for my birthday, my son Sam presented me with a beautifully framed picture of "Baschert." He had enlarged a photograph and created a three foot by two foot piece of art. The picture showed the wind filling the boat's five unfurled sails, clearly capturing its beauty. Over the years, the color faded giving the boat, clouds and water a unique and spectacular sepia appearance. It was an outstanding representation of the boat; I felt it might be effective in portraying its true worth. The IRS agent's job is to enforce the reduced deduction; our job is to convince him that the IRS is wrong and our value is correct. I conferred with my accountant and he agreed that by bringing the picture we had nothing to lose and everything to gain.

On the conference day, and taking the carefully wrapped picture, I met my accountant at the Federal building in downtown New York City. We proceeded to the designated room. Shortly, the door opened and a young man walked in wearing a "Kippah" (yarmulke), a skull cap worn by Jewish men. The "Kippah" is a religious symbol. "Payess," uncut sideburns, were wrapped around his ears. It was evident that he was an Orthodox Jew.

My accountant and I looked at each other and we did a double take. The fact that we were all Jewish could not hurt our cause. We rose. My accountant extended his hand and said, "Good morning. I'm Joshua Goldberg." Looking in my direction, he continued, "and I represent Dr. Stewart Crowngold in this matter." When he introduced us, the agent's brow furrowed and his eyes widened acknowledging the Jewish-sounding names. The concept of empathy within ethnic groups is universal.

The agent, Mr. Kronkite, shook Joshua's hand, pointed to our chairs and said, "O.K. Let's sit and get to da bottom of da problem." During the ensuing discussion, my accountant kept referring to the two appraisals which averaged $40,000 and the agent kept referring to the nautical Blue Book and its $8,000 valuation. The discussion was going in circles when Mr.

Kronkite said, "Listen! I know da limitations of da Bluebook. Maybe I got a little room to move. Based on d'upgrades and da boat's condition, maybe I can convince my boss a $12,000 deduction is O.K. Dat's da best I can do. I got a boss dat always looks over my shoulder." He wanted to bring the entire matter to a close with this frugal offer.

I looked at my accountant dismayed. The IRS agent was going to give me an additional $4,000 deduction? Was he kidding? Noting the incredulous look on my face, my accountant continued the negotiations, but the agent was adamant. We were going nowhere quickly. Until this point, I had not been part of the discussion. Suddenly, with a slightly elevated voice, I exclaimed, "Wait a minute! Just wait a minute!" I was trying to be dramatic. I slowly walked over to the picture previously positioned against the back of a chair. "Perhaps I can show you something that will change your mind, something that will clearly demonstrate that we are talking about a special boat." I stood by the wrapped picture, paused for a moment and then dramatically tore away the protective paper. "This is what we have been talking about. This is the boat we are discussing. I hope this gives you a better perspective of the beauty and distinctiveness of the boat. Seeing is believing."

The agent stared at the picture, fixated. "Oh, boy! Oh, boy!" he exclaimed while jumping out of his chair. "I ain't never seen such a boat. Maybe in da movies, but no place else. It's like it should be in a movie, like da movies dat has Errol Flynn as da guy jumping around da boat. Dat's really your boat? Dat's really da boat from da donation?" I could not believe his excitement.

"Noooo! . . . That's not my boat, . . . *that's my umbrella*! . . . Of course that's my boat! All along, we have been trying to explain to you that the boat is valuable and special and the marine estimates are correct."

For several moments, there was taunting silence in the room. Suddenly, the IRS agent interrupted the stillness and said, "Listen, listen." There was a long pause. He continued. "I never saw such a boat like dis. I'm sure I can justify da value and I'm gona allow d'original deduction. Boy oh boy, mista, dats some boat."

My accountant and I rose, shook his hand and thanked him for his decision. Without re-wrapping the picture, we quickly departed before he could change his mind. As we left, the IRS agent was still shaking his head in wonderment.

OF ALL THE THINGS WHICH WISDOM PROVIDES TO MAKE US ENTIRELY HAPPY, MUCH THE GREATEST IS THE POSSESSION OF FRIENDSHIP.

EPICURUS

**I AM NOT AFRAID OF TOMORROW,
FOR I HAVE SEEN YESTERDAY
AND I LOVE TODAY.**

WILLIAM ALLEN WHITE

**ENJOY THE LITTLE THINGS, FOR ONE DAY
YOU MAY LOOK BACK AND REALIZE
THEY WERE THE BIG THINGS.**

ROBERT BRAULT

Sixteen

Funny is not always fun

One day, I received a letter from a major international organization congratulating me for being selected runner-up to their "Man of the Year." Coming so close and not having won made me feel sad. However, there was another part of me that was elated because the person awarded this coveted honor was a close friend and someone I greatly admired. The disappointment of coming in second is dampened considerably when the winner is a good friend, a mentor, considerably older, and much more deserving. Realizing the members of the organization recognized only one person more highly suited for the "Man of the Year" accolade than me was my reward.

Beyond the felicitations, the letter also invited me to their black-tie awards banquet. It stipulated the organization would underwrite the dinner's cost for me and my wife and would pay for one night's stay at the hotel. Additionally, they indicated I would be recognized as the runner-up at the awards presentation.

The banquet was to be held on a Saturday night in a major Washington, D.C. hotel. My wife and I decided to make the trip and spend a weekend in the Capitol. Beyond the ceremonies and the dinner, this jaunt would offer us an opportunity to visit many sights we had never seen.

I answered the letter affirmatively and made arrangements for the trip. There was no requisite to rent a tuxedo. Early in my career, I realized the need for formal attire, so I purchased a tuxedo and all the accouterments. In the long run, this saved me a considerable amount of money. Should a tuxedo be necessary, it was available and the fit was always suitable (no pun intended) assuming I did not gain too much weight. It was conservative in style so it was always proper.

After each wearing, the tuxedo and ruffled shirt were taken to the cleaners, eventually to be returned to my closet to dangle, each on its own hanger, waiting to be used again. The tuxedo's bow tie, cummerbund, suspenders, cufflinks, and studs were kept in a separate box. On a moment's notice, all that had to be done was remove the two hangers from the closet and take the box with the accouterments.

With our clothes packed, we took the early morning shuttle to Washington, D.C. Flights left every hour on the hour, so a mad dash to the airport was not necessary. After landing at Regan Airport, we took a cab to the hotel. We checked into the hotel a little after noon, had lunch, and then took a walk. It was a lovely Spring day, and the few visible Apple trees were in full bloom; the blossoms were magnificent. It was late afternoon when we returned to the hotel, time to nap. Well, at least I napped. My wife watched television for a while then addressed some postcards she had purchased. The cocktail hour was designated for seven p.m., so we were not in a rush. We could start dressing at 6:30 p.m. and be in the ballroom at 7:15 p.m. We never liked to be first arrivals.

My wife woke me at 6:00 p.m. and I jumped into a hot shower, shaved, and did my hair. That sounds funny, but it was true. I had been losing hair at the front of my scalp for several years, resulting in a receding hairline. I combed my hair in such a manner that it would drape over and cover this increasing bald area. In other words, I no longer combed my hair, I arranged it. It remains today as one of the capitol's undisclosed coverups.

Having completed all the preliminaries, it was time to get dressed. I went to the closet and pulled out the two hangers holding my tuxedo and shirt. I put on fresh underwear and reached for my tuxedo pants under the protective cleaning store cover. There were no pants on the hanger, only the jacket. What the heck is going on here? Where are the pants? Perhaps my wife was playing some sort of joke on me? But that was not her style.

"Honey, have you seen my tuxedo pants?"

"What the heck would I be doing with your tuxedo pants?"

The pants always came back on the hanger with the jacket. Where the heck could they be? This is the first time they were dry-cleaned at the new cleaners. Perhaps the pants were returned on a separate hanger? If so, they were presently hanging in my closet in our apartment. What a helpful thought. What the heck do I do now?

My wife recognized my agitation and realized I was upset. I relayed all the information to her and she suggested I immediately call the concierge to find out if a haberdashery or tuxedo rental store might be open. The concierge gave me several telephone numbers to call and there was not a response from any of them. It was almost seven p.m., it was Saturday night, and they were all closed.

After pondering for a moment, I asked my wife to call the president of the organization to tell her that I would not be able to attend the dinner.

"Are you kidding," she replied? "It's your screw-up so

make the call yourself and dig yourself out of your own hole." Meanwhile, my wife was completely dressed and ready to go.

I dialed the president's number and, utterly embarrassed, recounted the entire story. I told her it would be impossible for me to attend the banquet and ceremonies without tuxedo pants. I would be mortified.

No more than ten minutes had passed when there was a knock on the door. I opened the door, and the President of the organization rushed in and said, "You must come. You are part of the program which has already been printed and dispersed. If you do not show up there will be too many questions and too few answers."

"As I said to you over the phone, I would be too embarrassed."

The President paused for a moment. "Look," she pleaded. "I know you are a professor at dental school and I understand you are a good teacher. Just think about what our students could learn from this. Our organization is primarily focused on learning disabled children who often misplace or lose things, especially items of clothing. You remember the classical joke about our children . . . a student walks into the classroom with one sneaker and the teacher asks if the student lost a sneaker? The student replies, 'nope, I found one.' Well think of the learning experience when they find out that even a big shot professor could lose, misplace, or not be able to find things. Think about what this type of exposure will do for them, for their self-confidence. You must attend the banquet. You must allow me to explain the error, and you will see how beneficial it will be for these youngsters."

The president was putting the pressure on me. Could I refuse her, given her argument? I agreed to attend wearing my tuxedo jacket and jeans.

After dressing, I looked at myself in the mirror. I definitely had a Greenwich Village look. A punk-rock 'do, green hair, and an earring or lip labret would have complimented my outfit.

Unfortunately, I had insufficient hair to do the punk-rock 'do, green hair would be too close a color to my complexion, and an earring or lip labret would conflict with the nose ring that came with my long term marriage commitment.

When I walked into the banquet hall, I met many people whom I knew. Many children had accompanied their parents. Nobody seemed to notice my "outfit," and if they did no comments were made. At the awards ceremony, the President described what had occurred, and called me to the podium. There were chuckles, titters, and snickers throughout the room and I received a long and loud applause. After the ceremonies ended, many children approached me with their own stories about losing or misplacing things. It was most rewarding knowing such a wonderful chord had been struck with so many of the kids.

Was the audience amused by my forgetfulness? Certainly. Did most of the participants laugh at my appearance? I think so. Was there a lesson to be learned from my folly? Without question, most attendees will be more cautious in their endeavors, at least for a while.

Yes, it was funny.

But did I have fun?

I think not.

EVERYTHING IS FUNNY AS LONG AS IT IS HAPPENING TO SOMEBODY ELSE.

WILL ROGERS

THE RAREST THING A MAN EVER DUZ IZ THE BEST HE CAN [SIC].

JOSH BILLINGS

Seventeen

Tongue twister

It was a warm summer's morning, the sun was rising and my teenage daughter and I were driving West on the Long Island Expressway (LIE), heading toward New York City. Though the LIE is a six-lane highway, it is often referred to as the world's longest parking lot because rush hour traffic is often bumper to bumper, especially, when approaching the Midtown tunnel. I have often thought a powerful truck pulling several connected cars could save motorists a great deal of stress and a large amount of gas. Depending upon the severity of the traffic, we would need two hours to arrive at my dental office from my home in Farmingdale, approximately thirty miles from the city.

The idea for this particular trip originated the previc·
when my wife suggested that our daughter Lois accc·
to my office. She knew one of my assistants w?

and felt Lois could help. My wife always sought a reprieve for our daughter from the summer's doldrums. Heaven forbid she should help clean the house or occasionally cook. It was summer vacation and Lois, a very bright young lady, was bored. What a wonderful idea, I thought. I certainly could use her assistance and I would have the added pleasure of spending time with the princess.

We immediately made plans on how to spend the day. Usually, I would travel on the Long Island Railroad to my office. Even though the railroad cars were cold in the winter, warm in the summer, generally dirty and noisy, I could still read the paper or nap depending on my mood. I never liked driving to the city alone because of the slow pace and no one to talk with, and this made me sleepy. I was concerned that I might fall asleep and cause an accident. My daughter's company convinced me to drive. Ultimately, this proved to be a very trying experience.

Our initial discussion centered around my daughter's wearing apparel; we decided nothing fancy, just clean and functional. We agreed to depart early in the morning. Without provocation, the princess could sleep well into the afternoon. She loved to read into the long hours of the night but was willing to give up this pastime to be relaxed and subsequently be better prepared for the next day. It was extraordinary for sleeping beauty to rise early. Of course, if she had to sacrifice, I did too. I normally rise early, so it followed that I would also go to bed early. I usually go to bed a little later if there is a good ball game on television. I expected this to be such a night, but my daughter convinced me to retire early. Her concluding argument was that if the game was so important, I could always tape it and watch it some other time. Smart young lady. The daughter does not fall too far from the mother tree.

I awoke the next morning to find my daughter dressed and ready to leave. She appeared to be wide awake but a little apprehensive. We decided to eat something light to tide us over until we arrived at the office. We could order egg sandwiches or some other delight from the many food stores located in the vicinity. Food delivery was not a problem. To induce Lois' cooperation in the office, the princess was told that in addition to a day's wages, lunch would be a bonus. My wife, suddenly an aspiring employment agent, tried to represent my daughter in these sensitive negotiations. It was decided to keep this strictly a business affair between my daughter and me without third party interference. The princess did not need any intermediary to get special compensation. My daughter felt I would reward her appropriately. After all, hadn't I always?

We jumped into the car, drove out of the neighborhood, and were soon on the LIE. A light conversation began and about fifteen minutes after our departure, my daughter turned to me and asked, "Dad, what am I supposed to do when we get to the office? How do I help you?" The princess was baffled!

I explained that she would do simple chores: dismiss the patient after I finished working; clean and sterilize the operatory; seat the next patient in the dental chair and place a protective cover on the patient so I could begin working immediately after entering the treatment room. Additionally, she could assist by bringing me the patient's chart. She was very bright and to relieve any anxieties, I expressed my confidence in her ability to surmount problems. I indicated her most important responsibility would be to answer the phone. She had unlimited training in this area gained from the hours she spent on the phone with her girlfriends.

Inquisitively, she asked, "Is there any special way you want me to answer the phone?"

"Yes," I replied. "With an authoritative but friendly voice say, Good morning, doctor's office, Lois speaking may I help you?" I told her there were variations. She could say "Doctor Jones' office" instead of just "Doctor's office" or say "this is Lois, may I help you?" instead of saying "this is Lois speaking."

Fortified with this information, my daughter began practicing. Suddenly I hear, "*GOOD* morning, doctor's office, this is Lois speaking, may I help you?" The emphasis was unquestionably on the word "*GOOD*."

"How did that sound, Dad?" she asked.

"Just fine."

"Good *MORNING*, doctors office, this is Lois speaking, may I help you?" She paused for a moment. "Was that any better," she inquired having put the emphasis on *MORNING*?

"Either way sounded OK to me," I replied.

For the next hour, she rehearsed, each time changing words or placing the inflection on different words. Doctor *JONES'* office, *DOCTOR'S* office, this is *LOIS* speaking. This is Lois speaking, may I *HELP* you. She repeatedly changed intonations. After a while her tonal changes sounded like the irritating blast of a car horn. I kept turning my head to see what was wrong on the road.

"Sweetheart," I said "your driving me crazy. I appreciate your practicing, but can't you whisper to yourself?"

"No, Dad," she said "I want it perfect and I can only do it by practicing out loud."

The rehearsal continued. If I had ear plugs, I would have certainly used them. I was driving, therefore I could only cover one ear at a time. I was going nuts.

After leaving the midtown tunnel, it was only ten minutes to my office. The rehearsals had ended, but the ringing in my ears continued. I parked the car and we walked to the office. Arriving, I suggested to Lois that she become familiar with the office, specifically the front desk, the appointment book, pens, pencils, and the phone. Meanwhile, I went to make coffee, a ritual in my office. When my assistants arrived in the morning, they knew a good cup of coffee was waiting. When they made coffee, it was exceptionally strong, tasted like bile, constricted your throat, and threatened to remove the enamel from your teeth.

After fifteen minutes, the moment of truth arrived: the phone rang. Would all the time spent rehearsing pay off? Holding a cup of coffee in my hand, I stepped into the office doorway to watch and listen. Lois picked up the phone, . . . "Good Doctor, MORNING'S office, this is Lois, do you need any help?" The cup of coffee fell out of my hand onto the floor. After all her rehearsing, after all my suffering during those rehearsals the princess goofed. I could not believe what I heard. It was testimony to the demon called anxiety which sometimes causes the most intelligent person to make a mistake.

Lois cleaned up the spilled coffee. After all, wasn't that part of her job description. From that moment, each time the phone rang her face became beet red, but she responded precisely as rehearsed, with dignity and poise. Whenever she was on the phone and I looked at her, she would comically stick out her tongue and make a face, a typical teenage gesture indicating she had mastered the task. Overall, my daughter had a marvelous day and so did I. She was extremely helpful and was rewarded handsomely (at least in my opinion).

When we returned home, the princess' mother attempted to renegotiate her non existent employment contract.

NOBODY CAN MAKE YOU FEEL INFERIOR WITHOUT YOUR PERMISSION.

ELEANOR ROOSEVELT

Eighteen

The telephone

Introduction

If you pick up a telephone receiver in our remarkable electronic age and do not press the buttons to make a call, within thirty seconds you will hear the message, "If you would like to make a call please hang up and try again." This was not the situation in the early 1970's. At that time, it would take a few minutes for the dial tone to alert you to dial the number or hang up. It was these few minutes that permitted the following extraordinary telephone exchange to play out.

The Stage

A small dental office with two dental operatories (rooms used by the dentist to operate on patients) at the end of a hallway, a hygienist's room whose doorway faces a receptionist's desk, a doorway to a laboratory down the hallway between the receptionist's desk and an operatory. The second operatory is offset from the hallway. There is a wall-mounted telephone on the common wall between the two operatories. Anyone using the telephone in this operatory could not be seen by the receptionist unless the caller stepped into the doorway.

The Players

Dr. Jones, the dentist, played by me; a hygienist played by Carol; a receptionist played by Janet; and a chair side assistant played by Maureen. The dentist is a big kibitzer and the receptionist is hard of hearing.

The Play

Doctor Jones completes work on a patient and the patient leaves. Doctor Jones is alone in the offset operatory and decides to make a phone call. The hygienist is working on a patient in her room and the receptionist is working at her desk. Maureen, the chair side assistant, is in the laboratory.

I pick up the receiver to make a call and hear my receptionist say, "Doctor Jones' office, how may I help you?" I realize immediately that the telephone receivers were picked up simultaneously. I am certain Janet has no idea that I am on the other end of the line.

"I vant to spik mit da Dokta," I reply using a heavy Jewish accent.

"What's your name, sir?"

"Don't tink by callink me 'sir' I'm gona treat you special. Just put da Dokta on da phone."

"Look sir, I can't put the Doctor on the phone unless I know your name and you tell me what the problem is. The Doctor is a very busy person."

Janet, who was trained by me, knew I would not answer a phone call unless I recognized the caller. She is a large framed, mature woman. Janet believes the reception area is her domain. She has no children but has developed a mothering complex about the office.

"I knowd he's a busy guy, dat's vy I vant to spik mit him 'cause if you vant sumtink done a busy guy shud get it."

"Again, sir, whom am I speaking with."

"I taut dat 'whom' was on second base and 'with' is in the outfield. I am 'who' and not gettink to first base mit you."

Though she frequently went to baseball games with her husband, this bit of baseball humor went over her head.

"Sir, if you do not tell me your name and the nature of your problem I will have to hang up."

"Dare you go callink me 'sir' again. Look, mine problem is I got a toot ake undt I need a gutt dentist. I hoid dis dentist is a gutt dokta so I vant to see him he should fix mine problem."

"Well at least I now know what the problem is; now tell me your name."

Janet was just doing her job, following office procedure. It wasn't fair, since I knew how she would respond before she uttered the words.

"Again mit da name. Are you tellink me dat if you don't get mine name da dokta von't take care from mine toot ake."

"We must have your name in order to make un appointment."

At this point I made a rumbling sound, clearing my throat.

"Are you choking?" my receptionist quickly inquired.

"No, demmit, I'm serious. Vat are you tawkin apointmnt? Are you tellink me I got a toot ake and I got to make me un apointmnt?"

"Well, sir . . ."

"Dare vee go again. Don't 'vell sir' me. I can't belief dat da dokta vould make me to stay in pain until I cud cum for an apointmnt. Dats krul. I can't belief he vould do such a tink, make me vait in pain for un apointmnt . . . Ven vould dis apointmnt be?"

"Let me look at the appointment book."

"Look in da apointmnt book. I taut dat gutt doktas saw people imediately ven dey ver in pain so I shud cum to da office now, yes?"

"No, you cannot come up to the office now. I must have your name and telephone number."

Janet goofed here perhaps because she was under stress which caused her to get upset. The office policy indicated that when a patient in pain called for an appointment, he was told to come to the office immediately. If he said he could not come to the office right now and asked for another time he was given the first available appointment, even if that was two weeks away. A patient in pain was to come to the office immediately or receive a regular appointment.

"Dare vee go mit da name undt now you vant mine phone number? Vy for?"

"Well what if the doctor has to leave the office because of an emergency. We would want to call you so you wouldn't make a trip for nothing."

"Don't vorry honey, he got me for un emergency so he don't got to leave no office to find one."

At this particular time I realized that Janet was facing away from the operatory doorway. I could tell that she was exasperated because the volume of her voice was intensifying. I decided to put down the phone and walk to the operatory doorway. Janet couldn't see me. Because she was hard of hearing, I decided to speak in my normal tone certain she would still think I was on the phone.

Standing in the doorway with the phone sitting on the counter top, I continued, "Vot do you mean stop me so I shudn't make a trip for nuttink. I'm downstairs calling from da phone from da lobby and I'm comink right up."

"Look sir, you cannot come up now. The Doctor is working on a patient and will not be able to see you for quite awhile."

This was not true. Another error on Janet's part, most likely due to tension and frustration. I was not working on a patient and patients with emergencies were always told to come to the office immediately.

At this point, Carol the Hygienist walks out of her treatment room and proceeds down the hall to the laboratory. She stands in the doorway next to Maureen and they silently become hysterical with laughter. They are not visible to Janet because she is facing the reception room which is away from the laboratory and offset operatory.

Suddenly, Janet turns and has a horrified look on her face. Her mouth is open and her lower lip is drooping. She puts down the telephone and screams, "What's going on here?"

With this outburst, Carol and Maureen begin to laugh out loud. I am bending over laughing violently. Arms akimbo, Janet's face reddens. She gives me the most frightening look I have ever seen. Daggers were streaming from her eyes. If looks could kill, Janet would be a murderess.

FACTS DO NOT CEASE TO EXIST BECAUSE THEY ARE IGNORED.

ALDOUS HUXLEY

NINETEEN

The Keys

For as long as I can remember I have been forgetful. While contemplating one task and then another, my first thought often evaporates. The ability to hold one piece of information in the mind while concurrently considering another is called symbolic mental manipulation. My ability to simultaneously manage disparate information is appalling. For instance, while taking out the garbage, I forget to close the window, an act I previously decided to do. I forget to perform this act until I am at the garbage can. Sometimes I feel like a beer bottle, empty from the neck up. My forgetfulness is disturbing; especially, when I am far from home and recall important papers left behind. On other occasions, I look for one object and retrieve another. It is extremely frustrating. Information, objects or actions are temporarily forgotten because my mind is diverted by additional information not necessarily relevant to my initial thoughts.

In the past, I employed different strategies to prevent sequence interruption or my proclivity to forget. I left notes in several places to serve as a reminder. This approach works well if you find the notes. Another strategy I employed was periodic repetition. This resulted in constantly walking around talking to myself. This method was unsuccessful, especially if I was busy. I would constantly forget to remind myself. Actually, I never forget. I just do not remember at the appropriate time.

The most successful strategy employed involved my keys. Searching for them, I would walk away with a wallet, quite disconcerting, especially when they sat next to each other. Occasionally, when I found the key, it was the wrong one and I could not get into my house or office. I solved this problem by putting all my keys on one ring. However, taking the wrong object continued to be exasperating. My wife often remarked that if an object is under my nose, I still will not find it. I believe this happens because of the size of my nose.

I decided to attach my key ring to one end of a gold chain. The opposite end would be secured to something that is with me wherever I go. Assuming I would not go anywhere without my pants, I felt the key ring would serve as the best connector.

The chain does not fall below my knees, but swings gracefully from a belt loop to its resting place within my pocket. The chain, with the attached key ring, is kept on top of a dresser with my money clip, wallet, and handkerchief. They are constant companions and can always be found lying together. Eventually the key chain became bulky, so I wrapped my handkerchief around the keys to prevent them from tearing a hole in my pocket. This overall plan worked exceedingly well.

The brain is capable of retaining a finite amount of data at any one time. Having a small brain means fewer pieces of information are retained. Having no brains, a frequent accusation of my wife, is self-explanatory. Now, I no longer need to remember where the keys are or which key to take. They are always attached to the chain and can be found among my money, wallet, and handkerchief unless they are attached to my pants. I cannot explain why connecting the keys to a chain improved my symbolic mental manipulation, but it did.

One day, while working at my desk at the university, I had the urge to empty my bladder. Rising from my chair, I hurried to the rest room. While standing at the urinal, fly unzipped, my mind clouded with thoughts, the door opened and in walked my boss.

Turning my head slightly, I acknowledged him, and he said in a very shocked tone, "What the hell are you doing?"

"What do you mean?" I responded, "it's fairly obvious."

"Really," he replied. "Then why are you standing at the urinal holding your keys in your hand? Have you discovered a new and unique way of urinating? Isn't it difficult for the urine to flow through the chain? Perhaps we should apply to the government for a grant to study the efficacy of this obviously untried method of peeing?" He was really spreading the sarcasm thick.

Looking down, I saw my unzipped fly and much to my chagrin, the set of keys in my hand. My overloaded brain had blocked out the purpose for my standing at the urinal. Day dreaming had caused my disability to again put me in an embarrassing situation. Luckily, I did not wet my pants. Maybe it is possible to urinate through a chain? I was mortified. My brain must have believed the chain was connected to my private parts and bypassed my first intention. While returning the keys to my pocket I looked at my boss, then nonchalantly emptied my bladder the conventional way. My face felt flushed, no pun intended. I had forgotten things before, but this had to be the most frustrating and embarrassing. While my boss stared, I calmly walked out of the rest room as though nothing had happened. He must have thought I was an idiot and I felt like an idiot! As I suspected, the story was told to everyone. For a while, the entire department had a great laugh. Fortunately, it did not make the front page of the New York Times.

**OUR DEEDS FOLLOW US,
AND WHAT WE HAVE BEEN
MAKES US WHAT WE ARE.**

JOHN DYKES

TWENTY

Language arts

An Asian man approaches the information officer at his neighborhood bank and inquires, "Why two day ago I cash Yen for 'melican dolla,' and today I cash same number Yen for 'melican dolla' and I get less 'melican dolla' today?"

"Fluctuation," responded the information officer.

"Fluc you too, round eye, 'melican pig'."

----------   ----------

The different sounds of foreign languages often cause misinterpretation of words resulting in inappropriate responses from the listener. Although unintentional, these responses are often comical and a source of embarrassment to both parties. The following story serves as an illustration.

Sal manned the information desk in a large office building where my dental practice was located. He served in that position for more than forty years and was familiar with most of the tenants in the building. Soon after I opened my dental practice we became friendly, but strictly on a business basis. We entered into a silent barter arrangement where he would refer patients to me whenever possible and I would take care of his dental needs.

One day, Sal called my office and told the receptionist a Japanese tourist desperately needed my help. He indicated the man was in the building, had a terrible toothache, and spoke little English. "Can you take care of this guy?" Sal inquired. My receptionist told Sal to send him to the office immediately and we would take good care of him.

When the door buzzer rang, I walked out to greet him. He was frail, short, and impeccably dressed. He wore round, black-rimmed metal glasses and had the stereotypical front tooth arrangement of a Japanese male, seen during World War II - flared and bucked. Whenever Sal referred patients to the office, we tried to make them feel they were receiving special treatment. We found this approach to be a good policy, both for Sal and the office.

I extended my hand to the patient in a friendly gesture and said, "Hello." He grasped my hand and bowed deeply from the waist. It is Japanese custom to bow as a sign of respect, with the deepest bow demonstrating the highest honor. This gentleman exceeded expectations. He bowed so low that his head almost hit the floor. What homage he showed me.

It was obvious he did not have a good command of the English language. Each time we would say something, he gave a quizzical look, hesitated, and then responded, "Ah so!" This was an indication he was absorbing and beginning to understand what was said. However, we were never quite sure. With hand gestures, we were able to direct him into the dental operatory.

Using pointing gestures and other hints, I was able to determine the painful tooth. When evaluating someone's pain, it is necessary to analyze certain signs and symptoms which allows for a differential diagnosis. I found the use of pigeon English to be most effective in determining which tooth was bothering the patient. I would use words like toothee, hurtee, bad, good, etc. to determine the quality and quantity of his pain. "Which toothee hurtee? It hurtee when sleep? It hurtee when eat?" These were some of my questions.

An x-ray corroborated the extent of the damage and I decided his tooth could not be saved. Using pigeon English and hand signs, I explained to the patient that his tooth had to be extracted. After several attempts at clarification, the Japanese man paused for a moment and then responded, "Ah so." He paused again, and then said, "Okey!"

The patient's tooth was anaesthetized. Working slowly and carefully, the tooth was extracted without difficulty. I sensed a moment of relief from the patient. Had he really understood my pigeon English and hand signs describing the extraction procedures?

I placed a compress over the wound site to stop any bleeding. After a suitable period, the site was examined and no further bleeding was discernable. Once again, using pigeon English, I explained to the patient the procedures to be followed to avoid any post surgical complications: no rinsing for four hours, cold compresses should be used if there was any swelling, etc. These instructions were given to the patient in written form. Unfortunately, they were in English. The patient was released and one of my assistants walked him to the receptionist's desk.

He faced the receptionist, bowed deeply and inquired, "How much for today?"

In her best pigeon English, my receptionist responded, "Sixty for today."

The Japanese man proceeded to write a check, handed it to my receptionist, bowed again and left the office.

As soon as the door closed, I could hear my receptionist and assistant begin to giggle. I walked to the front desk and asked what was so funny. Still giggling, my receptionist handed me the check the Japanese man had written.

I couldn't believe my eyes. The check was written in the amount of **. . . sixty-four dollars.**

The name of this Japanese tourist has long been lost from memory. Two weeks after the extraction of his tooth, and I assume coincidentally with the completion of his visit to the "marvels of America" as he called them, he returned to my office to once again thank me and to present me with two beautiful wooden Japanese dolls, a boy and a girl, that he had painted expressly for me. They presently sit on top of a low book case in my office and give me great pleasure each time I view them. They constantly remind me that language is an art that permits two people with limited commonality to converse and understand each other.

Twenty One

Maria

She was gorgeous. She had short, jet-black hair with matching ebony eyes, high cheek bones, fully contoured lips, and an olive skin complection indigenous to some Italians. When she smiled, her face lit up. She did not have a model's figure but appeared soft and well endowed. What others might describe as slightly overweight, was, to me, perfect proportion, breasts to waist to hips. All of these features were positioned on two long, shapely legs. She was definitely "eye candy."

Maria became a patient of mine in the 1960's. When she first walked into my office, my lower jaw almost hit the ground. If I had been wearing glasses, I certainly would have broken the lenses. I worked on Maria's teeth several times over a four or five month period and we developed an excellent rapport. She had been a professional entertainer, a singer who worked weekend gigs at weddings and Bar Mitzvahs. Having tired of this lifestyle, she presently worked as an airline stewardess.

One day while crossing 34th street in New York, I spotted a very attractive female walking toward me. I could not stop staring and as we approached each other it was apparent she was staring at me also. The closer she came, the more breathtaking she looked. She was beautiful. It was summer time, and women wore thin, abbreviated garments making themselves very alluring. It was difficult to avoid sizing these females up and down, front and back. Without doubt, while I was ogling her, she was ogling me. It was what might be called "ocular sex." We came nearer to each other and all of a sudden I realized it was Maria.

"Hi Maria," I said cheerfully. It was obvious she did not recognize me. "I'm Dr. Jones" I continued. "I guess you don't recognize me with clothes on."

She blushed, looked me up and down, and finally realized who I was. We stared at each other, both understanding what the other was thinking. It was a very pleasant meeting, especially for me, and made my month.

A couple of years later, micro miniskirts became the rage. Of course, some women should have avoided the new trend for anatomical reasons. It was most refreshing to view a woman with a well-proportioned figure, supported by long, shapely legs covered, or uncovered, by a micro miniskirt.

One day, Maria had an appointment with me, and as she was ushered into my office I realized she had embraced the new trend effectively. I was a tooth doctor but also a male, so when a good-looking female walked into my office, the last part of the anatomy examined was the teeth. I could examine her teeth when she sat in my dental chair.

Maria was impeccably dressed, looked ravishing, smelled deliciously, and was wearing a micro miniskirt. Wow! The total package was unbelievable. I am certain my staring embarrassed her but I didn't care. She gave me a big smile and a small hug. I sensed she realized that her appearance had enthralled me. She sat down, turned her head toward me, and gave me a demure, seductive smile. She knew she was turning me on and I was not complaining. It was a great feeling.

My assistant, who was oblivious to what was going on, walked into the room and "draped the patient." This procedure involves placing a plastic-backed paper towel over the patient's chest, under their chin, and securing this paper "drape" with a chain. The purpose of the plastic backing is to prevent the patient's clothes from becoming soiled by fluids penetrating through the paper. When extensive work is done, a plastic sheet is placed over the patient's body extending to or below the knees depending upon the height of the patient. These plastic covers tend to make patients very warm and often cause them to perspire. Because of this, we only used them when we were doing extensive dentistry. Considering the type of work to be done and that it was summer, I decided not to use the plastic drape on Maria. The micro miniskirt had no bearing on my decision.

After Maria was seated and covered with the paperbacked towel, I tilted the dental chair to place her in the prone position. This was done solely to position the patient so I could properly work on her teeth. The assistant was in the room and the door to the operatory was open. This was standard procedure. Maria relaxed in the chair. Despite the miniskirt, I noticed her legs were uncrossed. This was not embarrassing for Maria because I was seated behind her, she was facing the window, and my office was on the fifteenth floor. Minimally covered, Maria's legs were undeniably beautiful.

I began working on Maria's teeth and after a few minutes passed I noticed something out of the corner of my eye. I looked toward the window and spotted what appeared to be the top of a man's head. His hair was short, brown, and very windblown. What the heck was going on? This is the fifteenth floor. What is someone doing outside my window? As I stared out the window, the man's head slowly came more and more into view, his forehead now very evident. It suddenly occurred to me what was happening. This guy was on a rising scaffold working on the outside of the building. As I continued to watch, the man's eyes came into view and they immediately began to bulge. Oh my God, Maria was lying in my chair, in her miniskirt, legs spread wide apart facing the window.

As the scaffold rose, the man's face continued to unfold and soon I could see his lower jaw hanging down. He had an unbelievably amazed look on his face.

"Maria, Maria," I said hurriedly, with grave concern in my voice, "you better cross your legs."

"What are you talking about," she responded?

"You damn better quickly cross your legs because there's a man standing on a scaffold staring at your crotch. If you don't cross your legs soon, the view might make him so nervous he might lose his balance and fall."

Maria lifted her head slightly, stared at the unbelieving face in the window, repositioned her head on the dental chair, turned to look at me, and through a relaxed smile said,

"Let the son-of-a-bitch fall."

When I retired, Maria had been a patient of mine for almost thirty-five years. The last time I saw her she still had a beautiful face and a marvelous figure. On her fiftieth birthday, she had no wrinkles on her face and no parts of her anatomy sagged. We discussed her wonderful preservation despite her age. Perhaps it was because she never married and never had children. ¿Quién sabe?

**GREAT LOVERS, LIKE SCRIBES,
KNOW
IT IS NOT THE SIZE OF THE PEN
BUT THE PENMANSHIP THAT COUNTS.**

THE AUTHOR

Twenty Two

Amazing

My son Sid held a barbeque at his home to raise funds for his Temple. Among the assorted foods served were frankfurters, which he purchased on sale from the local supermarket for five dollars per package. After the barbeque, he stored the unsold packages of "dogs" in his freezer and called me to find out whether I wanted any. He mentioned they were bought at a "buy one, get one free" sale.

"Six packages would be enough," I replied. "I'll take them off your hands when I see you again." Naturally, I assumed I would pay for three packages.

A few weeks passed and finally he brought the hotdogs to my home.

"How many packages did you bring?"

"I only had five left," my son responded.

"So how much do I owe you?"

"They were five dollars a package, so you owe me twenty-five dollars."

"Wait a minute!" I exclaimed bewildered. "I thought you said they were 'buy one, get one' free."

"Yep, you're right. That's what I told you," he acknowledged. "But since I last spoke to you I ate the free ones. You owe me twenty-five dollars."

This situation reminds me of a saying I hear frequently: IF YOU CAN'T BEAT'EM, CHEAT'EM.

**TIME IS A GREAT TEACHER,
BUT UNFORTUNATELY
IT KILLS ALL ITS PUPILS.**

HECTOR BERLIOZ

TWENTY THREE

Black and brown

They were young, handsome, well dressed, talented, and on their way to the pinnacle of success. Both were patients in my dental practice. It was the summer of 1965. Bill and David, who were in their early thirties, shared an apartment on the upper East Side of New York City primarily to divide the high rent and thus enable them to cope with other expenses. A good address is helpful in meeting the right people in their quest for success. They had much in common. Bill was an attorney, a junior partner in a prestigious law firm and on the inside track to a full partnership. David was a writer who just published his first novel, which won the Houghton-Mifflin Literary Fellowship Award.

In the late 1950's, David was a member of Lyndon B. Johnson's senatorial staff. Johnson became Vice President in

1960. After President Kennedy's assassination in 1963, David accompanied Johnson to the White House. When Johnson ran for reelection in 1964, David served as one of his speech writers and advance personnel, preceding the President on his stumps around the country. On several occasions, my secretary walked into the treatment room and said "David, the White House is on the phone." We often heard David respond to the caller on the other end: "Yes, Mr. President" or "No, Mr. President." When this occurred, everything stopped. We had a prestigious patient in our office.

David arrived on time for his appointment. The first patient of the morning, he was quickly seated in my treatment chair. We chatted for a bit and then I noticed he was wearing two different colored shoes, one black and one brown. I began to chuckle and he asked me what was so funny?

"Well, I don't want to embarrass you," I replied, my eyes staring downward, "but you are wearing two different colored shoes." I quickly added, "at least they are on the correct foot." With that comment, I again began to laugh softly.

David quickly glanced downward at his shoes and began chuckling. "I'll tell you what's so funny Doc.," David said. "It's a course of events that makes me smile even as I speak." His Southern drawl was most charming. "It is a beautiful day outside and having risen earlier than usual and suspecting I would be early for my appointment with you, I decided to walk here from my apartment. While strolling, I spotted a shoeshine 'boy' opening his stand. I use the word 'boy,' but he was actually a much older man, if you know what I mean."

I understood exactly that by referring to the older man as "boy" he was Black. David had made several bigoted remarks during the course of his many visits to my office. "Anyway," he continued, "his stand was located on the corner of the block, leaning against the bricks of a sizeable building. It sat on a large piece of red carpet, probably to increase the stand's noticeability. I computed there was adequate time for a shoe shine until my appointment with you, so I waited while he opened his stand. The streets were beginning to fill with people scurrying to work. The accompanying noise got louder and louder, affecting the quiet of the morning. As I watched, he lifted the heavy, waterproofed cover from the stand, then removed a yellow polka-dotted oil cloth from one of the drawers and wrapped it around his waist. He secured the apron to his body using a piece of rope which he tied behind his back."

"Waitin' for a shine mister?"

"I nodded my head, and the 'boy' quickly handed me the morning newspaper and said,"

"Y'all hop in the chair then."

"I took a big step up, climbed into a large, black leather chair, and placed my feet firmly on the pedestals. The riser is much higher on a shoeshine stand, so getting to the chair is never easy. Before I could open the newspaper, the 'boy' said to me,"

"There's two kinds a shine y'all can have, mister. A spit shine, which'll cost y'all two dolla', an' a hard shine, which'll cost y'all fo' dolla'."

"When I asked him what the difference was, he responded, probably for the millionth time, 'two bucks'."

"I opened the newspaper and began reading the news. I could hear him humming while rummaging through the stand's drawers obviously looking for the rags, brushes, and shoe polish he needed. I heard him mumble something about working at a shoeshine stand always keeps you moving. After a short while he paused, then asked whether I wanted black or brown polish? I could not believe what I heard. What a dumb question. Perhaps it was another attempt at humor."

"Slowly lowering the newspaper to the tip of my nose so I could see the face of the 'boy,' I remarked sarcastically, 'Why the heck don't you use your pea-sized brain and figure out what color to use, unless you have something against Black?' I was certain I had put on a pair of black shoes."

"Yasah, boss."

"There was a sarcastic tone to his response. I returned to reading the newspaper and I could feel the 'boy' apply the polish to the shoes, brush them, and then strop them with a cloth. He repeated the sequence, and then I heard a spitting sound and instinctively knew which type of shine I was getting. When he was done, he tapped the sole of one of my shoes, the classical method of informing the customer the shine was finished. The shoeshine 'boy' stepped back. I stepped down from the stand, paid the 'boy' and continued my walk here. It wasn't until you told me I was wearing one black shoe and one brown shoe that I knew. It certainly explains why the 'boy' wanted to know which color I preferred."

There was a short pause, and then David became hysterical and uncontrollable with laughter. I could not understand what was so funny. Finally, David calmed down, looked at me, began to giggle, and then answered my curiosity. "You know my roommate, Bill, don't you? I believe he's a patient of yours?"

"Sure I do. He's an attorney, right?"

"That's him," he continued. "Well, Bill and I live together, we're very much the same height and weight, and we often interchange our clothing. Even our shoe size is the same." David paused abruptly and then slowly continued, "Between the two of us, we only own two pairs of shoes, one black and the other brown . . . I wonder if Bill knows?"

David once again became hysterical.

TWENTY FOUR

Serendipity

The name was unfamiliar, so I asked my receptionist for information about my next patient. "He called bright and early this morning," she responded. "His name is Carlos Huerta. The right side of his face is swollen and he's complaining of pain. He should be here shortly. By the way, I had to cancel Mr. Kelly to get him in at eleven."

Our office policy provides that immediate attention is given to emergency cases even if it requires canceling a regularly scheduled patient. If the caller cannot make the proposed appointment, an alternate time is offered predicated on my availability. I am willing to disrupt my schedule to accommodate an emergency. However, the caller must accept the time slot offered and not expect an appointment predicated on his convenience.

"Do you know anything about him?" I inquired.

"Well, he's from Mexico, visiting New York. He's staying at a fancy, expensive hotel. I forgot the name. Oh! Something else. He was referred by your cousin Alan, the head of security."

At first, I did not recall a relative named Alan. Suddenly, I remembered it wasn't my cousin. It was my wife's cousin. Alan served as a Military Policeman in World War II and following his Army discharge joined the New York City Police Department. After retiring, he became the head of security at the Seasons Hotel. Alan was six feet, two inches tall, had fiery red hair with a temper to match. He loved to talk. When he caught someone in a traffic violation, he chatted with them at length, and they still received the ticket. His conversation was so delightful, it took the sting out of receiving the citation. While on the police force, he received several commendations for valor and now probably made an excellent head of security. The referral of Mr. Huerta to my office was a fortunate stroke of serendipity as we shall see.

Precisely at eleven a.m. Mr. Huerta, accompanied by an impeccably dressed, beautiful, mature woman, walked into my office. A large, magnificent pear-shaped diamond ring decorated the woman's finger. Mr. Huerta appeared to be in his early sixties though she seemed much younger. She was gorgeous! I later discovered they were childhood sweethearts, married, and approximately the same age.

After completing the usual medical form, Mr. Huerta was escorted into the dental operatory. He was relatively short, perhaps five-feet, five-inches tall, had typical Mexican bronze skin color and wore glasses. Because of the facial swelling, the eyeglass lens on the right side of his face sat higher than the one on his left, creating a comical appearance.

After introducing myself, I asked him several pertinent questions. From his responses, in perfect English, I concluded he had an abscessed tooth. An x-ray confirmed my suspicion.

I carefully explained two possible treatment plans. The first was to extract the tooth, which I did not recommend. This procedure could not be undertaken until the infection was eliminated by antibiotics. The second, the preferred procedure, was to save the tooth. This necessitated taking an antibiotic and then drilling a hole into the tooth's nerve canal to allow the abscess to drain. The pain and swelling would disappear and later the tooth could be saved by doing root canal in Mexico.

He agreed to try saving the tooth and was given a preliminary antibiotic. When I picked up the dental drill Mr. Huerta, alarmed, shouted,

"Wait a minute!" He attempted to grab my hand that held the drill. I pulled it away quickly. He grumbled, "Aren't you going to give me a shot?"

"An abscess causes the nerve to die. Dead nerves cannot cause pain. Therefore, a shot is not necessary," I explained. "You may feel some pressure but you will *not* feel any pain."

His jaw tightened with concern and he asked, "Doc, how does the nerve know it's dead? Are you sure?"

"I don't know *how* the nerve knows," I replied. "The only important thing is *the nerve knows* it's dead."

He was tense and his face was creased with apprehension. I began drilling and he suffered no pain or discomfort other than from his anxiety. I prescribed additional antibiotics as part of the treatment to resolve the infection. I advised him that the pressure and facial swelling should disappear within twenty-four to forty-eight hours. Additionally, there were no medical restrictions if he wanted to fly back to Mexico. He was strongly advised to see his dentist in Mexico immediately on his return.

After that discussion he appeared relaxed and pleased, and mentioned the pressure on his face was diminishing. Then he inquired if I did root canal treatment and, if so, would I treat him. I answered, "yes," but noted it could take several visits. Additionally, I alerted him to several other oral problems. His entire mouth needed treatment and it would be impractical to work on one tooth while others deteriorated. He asked for an overall dental evaluation and offered to remain in New York until it was completed.

A careful examination of his teeth was done and a full series of x-rays was taken. This was accompanied by impressions for study models. Usually, a review of the data and completion of an evaluation took a minimum of one week. However, due to his unique situation Mr. Huerta was given a follow up appointment in two days.

At the consultation, I gave him a comprehensive review of his dental health: present problems, problems that might occur in the future, and how they could be remediated or prevented. Most of his prior dentistry was poor bordering on the primitive. The abscess was the initial indication of his failing oral health. He required comprehensive rehabilitation treatment or eventually he would experience considerable problems in the future. The treatment would require numerous visits, would take months to finish and was extremely expensive. At this point, I did not know the extent of Mr. Huerta's wealth though this would not have made a difference.

On his return for the consultation, he was again accompanied by his wife. This pattern continued throughout the course of his treatment. On several occasions, he came alone. In these instances, before we finished, she always arrived carrying several packages, the fruits of her shopping spree.

Mr. Huerta noted that on the way to our appointment, he again met Alan who raved about my dental abilities. My cousin mentioned that I was a professor at the New York University College of Dentistry. I explained that I did not know how my cousin learned of my brilliance. Furthermore, I was only an instructor and not *yet* a professor. Mr. Huerta looked at me for a moment, then smiled. He must have thought a modest man is a talented man. With the facial swelling gone, he no longer had a comical appearance. He removed a billfold from his inside jacket pocket and counted ten unfolded, fresh five hundred dollar bills and placed them into my hand. I had never seen a five hundred-dollar bill and surely never had ten of them in my hand. "Is this deposit sufficient for what you proposed to do?" he inquired. My fee was quite substantial and I replied that the amount was an excellent beginning. My family had just moved into a new home and we needed furnishings. Thankfully, the money was not in pesos. It represented approximately 25 percent of the final fee.

Mr. Huerta was reminded that frequent trips and extended stays would be necessary to implement the treatment. At least one full week each month, and if everything went well the rehabilitation would be completed in approximately six months. I explained that the emergency therapy on his tooth should keep him trouble-free. Fortunately, he did not have to see his dentist on his return home.

The following week, Mr. Huerta called from Mexico and set up a series of appointments. I felt elated that he selected me to be his dentist. Equally exciting was the fee, the largest I had received to date. Additionally, it was an ego boost for me. I would be working on a wealthy international patient who would fly from his country to the U.S. to have his dentistry done.

Over the next several months, we became friends and had many discussions on political, social and historical matters. On one occasion, I learned of his background which was remarkable and would make a good movie.

Carlos' ancestors, holding a Spanish land grant, came to northern Mexico in the early eighteen hundreds. Initially, the family business was cattle and farming. Most wealthy Mexicans made investments in large agricultural estates; it was the only stable, productive enterprise and labor was cheap. Political disruptions, civil wars, unstable currency and the threat of banditry in the countryside were a constant problem. Agriculture was the only safe investment in those chaotic times. Over the years, the Huerta family amassed sizeable tracts of land and wealth.

Carlos was born in the beginning of the twentieth century.

Because of inferior Mexican schools, he was sent to private boarding schools in Texas. Subsequently, he attended college in Louisiana where he studied agricultural development. Carlos was the eldest son and after his graduation he was put in charge of the family's agribusiness. Besides cattle, the primary farm product was strawberries. Before graduating college, the only thing Carlos ever put on strawberries was sugar and cream: now it was fertilizer. Carlos was ambitious and an entrepreneur. He saw the financial rewards of expanding the business to incorporate increased production, diversification and distribution. He also recognized the need to develop other crops and products. In northern Mexico where his diverse produce was sold there were few supermarkets, so naturally, he built several and then selected his brother to manage this facet of the business. He increased corporate profits by establishing a trucking company to transport his produce to market. Another brother was put in charge of this enterprise. His youngest brother was responsible for running the family's oil and gas company. Next, Carlos established a bank. The profits of the combined enterprises were loaned to other entrepreneurs at the appropriate interest rate. Carlos appeared to be the Mexican J.P. Morgan and Andrew Carnegie combined. Finally, Carlos took a job: president of the bank. He told me that all these companies were created so his brothers and their families would be assured a comfortable income. After putting this conglomerate together, he now had time to spend the profits, a task he did with abandon. Amid all these accomplishments, Carlos and his wife found time to travel all over the world, except Russia.

Mr. Huerta's dentistry was completed without complications and he was extremely satisfied with the results. Afterwards, Carlos returned to New York twice a year to have his teeth cleaned and examined. He always stayed at least one week. According to him, the length of his visit was determined by the possible need for additional dentistry. However, I believe the true reason was to shop in New York's prestigious stores.

Although his hacienda was in northern Mexico, he maintained an apartment in Mexico City and felt shopping in that city was not comparable to what was available in New York.

On a few occasions, he made appointments with me for his son and daughter. More beautiful than the mother, the daughter could easily have decorated the cover of a high fashion magazine.

His son had the physical attributes of a movie star. Tall, with a bronze complexion and jet black hair, he also had the stereotypical black moustache of many Mexican actors. My female assistants were mesmerized by his attractiveness. In addition to his extraordinary good looks, we later learned of his athletic prowess. He won an equestrian team bronze medal in the Pan American games and represented Mexico in the Olympics in the same sport. Though Mr. Huerta's son and daughter were occasionally my patients, strangely, never Carlos' wife. Indeed, this was a unique family.

When Carlos appeared at my office for his semiannual evaluation in the Spring of 1982, he made an unexpected proposal to me. "We know each other almost twenty years," he said. "You have met my entire family and have been very professional and most gracious. I own a condominium in Acapulco and would like to invite you and your wife to come to Mexico as my guest. All you have to do is get there and I will take care of the rest." He did not include the airfare which proves you cannot have everything.

What a marvelous proposal! Initially speechless, I graciously replied that I must discuss his generous proposal with my wife and I would call him in a few days.

Returning home that evening, I told my wife, Bella, about Carlos' offer. She agreed it was most generous and gracious but declined to go. Having previously been to Acapulco, my wife was not impressed by it and she hated the heat. Furthermore, Bella felt strongly about the injustice of the homeless lying in the streets and the general squalor of the area. She urged me to go, insisting that the rest and relaxation would be good for me. The following day, I made arrangements with Carlos. I purchased a round trip ticket and early one afternoon found myself unwinding as my plane landed at Acapulco Airport.

As previously arranged, Carlos picked me up at the airport. Spotting me, he quickly called a porter, pointed out my bag and said, "Tome por favor esta bolse a mi coche." (Please take this bag to my car). He directed the porter to a large, black, four-door car with extremely wide whitewall tires. I could not understand why so many people were inspecting the car. To me it was not overly impressive. I later learned it was the largest car a Mexican citizen could legally own. Normally, the owner of such a car was rich or famous. Carlos probably belonged in both categories.

"Si, jefe," (yes, boss) responded the porter as he quickly picked up my suitcase. He followed us to Carlos' car and put the bag into the trunk. After tipping him Carlos said, "Come, let's go" and we sped away.

The trip to the center of Acapulco was uneventful. While driving we chatted about the plight of the poor Mexican peons. Carlos explained that because of the hotel industry there was a budding middle class emerging in Acapulco and he felt this was good for Mexico. Shortly, we arrived at the Acapulco Princess Hotel, the location of his condominium. He parked the car in a spot marked "reserved - Mr. Huerta." This was impressive. Although the condominium was very large, there were only two other reserved parking signs and they were not named.

"Come, let's say hello to my wife so she will know we have returned."

Once in the condominium, we took an elevator to the top floor. It was the penthouse and belonged to Carlos. The rooms were unbelievably large and magnificently decorated, with ceiling to floor glass windows on three sides offering views of the town, the mountains and the Gulf of Mexico. The panorama was extraordinary.

After greeting his wife, we had drinks and spoke for several minutes. Noticing I was tired, Carlos suggested that I go to my apartment to rest and clean up before dinner. I assumed I would stay in his place. In a sense, this was true. However, he escorted me to a beautifully decorated three room apartment on a lower floor and told me it was mine for the week. Carlos was magnanimous both in his invitation to visit him and my living quarters. Apparently, he recognized my need to relax and felt I should have my own rooms for privacy. It had no extraordinary view, other than of the Acapulco Princess. My dental background taught me never to look a gift horse in the oral cavity. He owned this apartment and kept it for guests. In the event I needed something and Carlos was unavailable, I was to find the building administrator. I suspected this was the superintendent. Give the person a title and you can pay him less.

Dinner was set for seven o'clock and he suggested we meet downstairs in front of the building at six forty-five. He then left. It was five o'clock.

After meeting, we walked across the parking lot to the Acapulco Princess' dining room. Wherever we went, Carlos was instantly recognized and greeted cordially and with reverence. "Buenos noches, el Sr. Huerto." (Good evening, Mr. Huerta), "La noche agradable, señor." (Nice night, señor), "Hava una cena buena, patrón." (Have a good dinner, patrón), were some of the salutations. The Spanish word "patrón" means boss, master, host or landlord. The term is employed in recognition of a person held in high esteem because of social status and wealth. From the tone in their voices, it was obvious that Carlos was respected and held in high regard.

The food and service were exceptional. After dinner, we returned to the condo and continued our conversation.

"Is eight o'clock too early for breakfast?" Carlos asked. "If not, why don't we meet where we just had dinner?"

"The time is acceptable," I replied and wished him and

his wife "buenas noches," a good evening. During dinner, he mentioned they were accustomed to going to bed early.

The next morning after breakfast, he took me on a tour of Acapulco. We spent most of the day driving through the countryside stopping for lunch at about noon. Carlos did not treat his servants as subordinates but was most generous to people. Wherever we went, people recognized him and paid their respects. He remarked that he received good service and attention by being kind and by giving appropriate monetary rewards. That evening we had dinner at a very upscale restaurant overlooking the city. Carlos' beautiful wife accompanied us. We spoke mainly about my impression of Acapulco. Again, everything was meticulously prepared as though for dignitaries.

As dinner was ending, Carlos delivered some startling news. Unfortunately, his bank in northern Mexico was part of a national crisis. After breakfast, he had to return home and deal with the problem. During his explanation, I felt the color drain from my face. He noticed my reaction and continued. "Nothing will interrupt your stay. The apartment is yours to use and my car is at your disposal. If you need anything, just ask the condominium administrator and he will make the arrangements. Please continue having your meals at the hotel and the charges will be put on my bill. When it is time to leave, the administrator will drive you to the airport and then return my car here. I am very sorry this happened. Are these arrangements alright?"

I offered my regrets about his problems and extended my thanks for his gracious hospitality.

"By the way Stewart," he had been using my first name for a long time, "after breakfast would you drive my wife and me to the airport? By doing so, you will have the car for your return to the condominium."

"Of course," I replied. "It would be my pleasure."

After breakfast, we left for the airport. I asked for the departure time and Carlos smiled and said "Don't worry, the flight will leave when I arrive." This confused me. Perhaps they do things differently in Mexico. On our approach to the airport he directed me to a side road. Suddenly, I was driving on the runway tarmac. I continued for about one-quarter mile and spotted a private plane. I understood his lack of concern about a departure time. It was Carlos' private jet. "Wow! Carlos owns a jet or perhaps it is a rent-a-jet? Who cares? " I said to myself. I was impressed!

After the luggage was placed on board, we said our goodbyes. By the time I returned to the car, the plane had taxied to the end of the runway waiting to take off. Rich or poor it's certainly nice to have money.

I returned to the condo. For the remainder of the week, each day I had brunch at the hotel and spent the afternoons lounging at the pool. A cocktail or two during the day helped me relax. The hotel employees knew I was Mr. Huerta's special guest and treated me accordingly. I was beginning to feel like one of the rich and famous.

I learned of the many excellent ethnic dining places in town: Italian, Spanish, French, and even Chinese were represented. Each evening, using directions received from the concierge, I drove Carlos' car to a different restaurant. During these excursions, the scene was always the same. When I arrived, a crowd of street urchins was always waiting, begging for pesos. These homeless children were filthy, their bodies caked with mud, their clothing torn and their feet shoeless. The sight made me cringe. How could a society allow its children to live in such squalor? Shame!!! This was one reason my wife refused to come. Wherever I parked, these youngsters would walk around and touch the car, while thinking here was a wealthy gringo.

"Ah, lo que un hermoso coche," (Wow, what a beautiful car) exclaimed one kid. "Es usted un norteamericano rico?" (Are you a rich American?) asked another. Almost always, the biggest kid in the group would shout, "Querria usted que mi proteger su coche, señor, y lo asegurarse no es rasguñado?" (Would you like me to protect your car, señor, and make sure it doesn't get scratched?) As a former street person from New York, I recognized this as a hustle, the protection racket. It upset me, but I could not take a chance; this was not my car. I always asked the "vocal one" if he spoke English. Invariably, the answer was "un poco," (a little).

"O.K., now listen carefully." I removed a twenty-peso bill from my pocket. It had great value for him but little value in American money. As he watched, I tore the bill in half. In my best pigeon Spanish I said, "Kid! See, one-half twenty pesos. If you do good, protect car, I give you other half. Comprende? One-half bill no good. Need both parts. I have 'mucho' pesos. You want other half of twenty peso bill? Protect car, make sure no damage, you get other half of bill and have twenty pesos. If car is damaged, I find you and you will get 'mucho legrimas de cocodrilo' (many crocodile tears). Comprende usted todo?" (Do you understand everything?). Using these few Spanish words made me feel confident the kid understood me. My two years of high school Spanish finally paid off. When returning to the car, I always felt relieved finding it still there and undamaged.

There is a feeling of loneliness being away from home. One evening, I found myself having dinner with Beatrice, Carlos' beautiful daughter. She drove from Mexico City to Acapulco unaware her parents were at their hacienda. We were at a lovely, outdoor French restaurant. The soft music was enchanting, and our half-filled wine glasses sparkled in the dwindling candlelight. Her hair fell around her shoulders in a curtain of auburn silk. The cool evening breeze stirred the loose strands of her hair and they undulated to the rhythm of the music. She was radiant and moonlight reflected from her large, dark eyes. Her perfume tantalized my very essence, stimulating erotic sensations. It was euphoric.

Moments later, we were in my room. A smile curved her sensuous lips. I stared into her warm, captivating eyes; her gaze locked on mine. I put my arms around her and her skin felt soft and velvety. She returned my affectionate embrace and whispered hushed sounds of pleasure in my ear. I was drowning in her intoxicating mystique. I kissed her with a violence and passion that culminated from all my earlier thoughts. Assaulted by exciting sensations, my senses spun wildly. I could feel her heart thumping madly against my chest. She molded her sensual body against mine. I was drowning in need, the demands of my body driving me closer and closer to the point of no return . . . Suddenly, the loud noise of a shutting door in the hallway woke me up. I smiled and realized that my wonderful vacation would soon be over.

At the end of the week, the building administrator drove me to the airport. There was no private jet waiting for me. I left Mexico through the regular airline. My stay in Acapulco was splendid. Ah, to live the life of the rich and famous.

Back home, I returned to my normal, mundane routine. I dropped Carlos a note thanking him for his gracious hospitality and mentioned that a surprise waited for him and his wife on their returned to New York.

When he came to my office, I proposed to take him and his wife to the Russian Tea Room, a very fine restaurant specializing in authentic Russian food. I knew they had never been to Russia and thought this might be exciting for them. Being of Russian descent, I had dined there several times and could testify to its authenticity.

Carlos and his wife seemed very pleased with this culinary treat. After they left, I rented a limousine and my wife and I were driven to Carlos' hotel. Waiting outside, Carlos and his wife were surprised at the sight of the limousine. They got in the car and Carlos proceeded to look everywhere and touch everything. He caressed the ashtrays, the glasses and bottles of liquor, even the ice bucket and the ice. His wife also noticed everything, but was more restrained. For the first time, he reverted to his native language. "Ah, es tan hermoso y tan grande." (Oh, it is so beautiful and so big.) He paused for a moment. "Y la mirada cómo todas las gafas y el licor extravagantes decantors . . . Y mira, nuestra radio personal." (And look how it has all the fancy glasses and liquor decanters . . . and look, our personal radio.)

"Cuán hermoso!" (How beautiful!) "Yo nunca he estado en un limousene antes. Esto es mi primer tiempo. Yo me siento como una virgen." (I have never been in a limousine before. This is my first time. I feel like a virgin.) With that remark, his wife blushed. It gave me great pleasure introducing a multimillionaire to something he never had.

Inside the restaurant, Carlos and his wife tried several Russian dishes: different caviars, herring, borscht, blintz and blini. They also had their fair share of Vodka, especially Carlos. All night, they constantly thanked me and my wife for a wonderful evening. It warmed our hearts.

Each time I saw Carlos, he again thanked me profusely for the wonderful evening at the Russian Tea Room. A few years later, he showed me pictures of the college he was building in northern Mexico. It was established to help educate less fortunate students and provide low tuition and scholarships. The school was dedicated to advancing and elevating the status of his people. Now in his eighties, he was still actively involved in many interests. This was the last time I saw him. Carlos was truly a "patrón" and the only one I have ever known.

BY FAILING TO PREPARE, YOU ARE PREPARING TO FAIL.

BENJAMIN FRANKLIN

Twenty Five

Unintended consequence

My secretary barged through the door. "Look," she shouted, "look at what I just bought." She briskly walked to her desk, tipped over her shopping bag, and emptied it onto the desktop. The contents seemed to be calculators, lots of them, and all appeared to be identical.

"You will not believe this," she said, every word exuding excitement. "There's a guy downstairs selling these calculators for five dollars apiece. Can you believe that? These calculators usually sell in stores for at least twenty-five dollars each and I got them for five. I was so excited, I bought a dozen."

The calculators looked beautiful and were easily worth five dollars . . . if they worked. "Are you sure they function?" I asked, "There are many con men lurking the streets and I suspect this is a con."

"You're always putting a damper on things," my secretary

replied. "I'm sure they work. The guy even showed me they work."

"Let me ask you one question," I responded. "Did he demonstrate using one of the calculators you bought or did he use one that he already held in his hand?"

"There you go again," she said. My secretary turned pale for a moment and was visibly upset. "Can't you believe it possible to get a bargain in this world?"

"Sure it's possible, but your purchase seems too good to be true." I paused for a moment and then continued, "Look! Try some of the calculators, show me they work, and shut me up?"

"That's the best idea since pay toilets," she replied.

My secretary picked up one of the calculators and started punching in numbers. She punched in two times four. "See," she said. "Eight," and she thrust the calculator in front of my eyes. I watched as she punched in six times six. "Look! Thirty-six." She quickly punched in three times seven. "Twenty-one. How's that? I told you it was a great deal."

"Keep going until you have used every number," I shot back at her. "Don't forget the plus and minus signs . . . and don't forget division and multiplication."

She punched in nine minus eight. "See! One," she said, showing me the screen.

Six plus nine was next. "Fifteen," she said. "Believe it now?" She was getting more and more contentious.

She then punched in five plus five and without looking at the screen shoved it in front of my eyes.

"Hold the calculator," I cried out. "Where I live, five plus five does not equal five."

She looked at the screen and instantly the color drained from her face. She became flustered and rattled. Without hesitation, and with a quivering urgency in her voice, she said, "Let's try it again." The answer again came up five. Whenever the number five was used, whether it was for addition, subtraction, division or multiplication, the resultant was always five.

"Looks like you found a great bargain," I said sarcastically. "Nine out of ten numbers work and, percentage wise, that's great. A baseball player getting nine hits in every ten at bats would become the world's greatest hitter. On the other hand, successfully crossing the street nine out of ten times without getting hit by a car is not necessarily reassuring. One small suggestion. When you have to use the number five, try another calculator."

As I walked out of the room, my secretary began checking each calculator. All that could be heard was the sound of plastic hitting the metal wastebasket.

IMAGINATION IS MORE IMPORTANT THAN KNOWLEDGE.

ALBERT EINSTEIN

**THE FUNCTION OF WISDOM IS TO
DISCRIMINATE BETWEEN
GOOD AND EVIL.**

ANONYMOUS

**YOUTH IS A BLUNDER;
MANHOOD A STRUGGLE;
OLD AGE A REGRET.**

BENJAMIN DISRAELI

TWENTY SIX

The swimmer

Thunderstorms were predicted for later in the day so, like previous forecasts, I took my umbrella to work. Adverse weather conditions are usually not challenging because it rarely rains when I carry an umbrella. However, without one a downpour is inevitable. It becomes a win-win situation. If carrying an umbrella prevents rain, that is beneficial; if it rains, I am prepared. In either case I will be carrying an umbrella, so the manufacturer is the ultimate winner.

On a clear, bright, sunny morning, toting an umbrella always makes me feel conspicuous. So, disregarding my feelings, rain prevention not rain expectation determined whether carrying an umbrella was viable. Such are the vagaries of life.

I expected the galley proofs of my first book to be delivered to my office today. I experienced an exceptional euphoria and I refused to allow anything to rain on my parade. It was a special moment to be shared with my patients and staff.

For the past thirteen years, I had taught at the dental college. In spite of the many new advances in concepts and materials during that time, there was no change in the departmental textbook. Two colleagues volunteered to help me write a new textbook. The responsibility of assembling the necessary collaborative pictures and relating them to the appropriate prose in the book was delegated to me. It was a time consuming and a tedious endeavor, taking almost two years to complete. But it was a labor of love. Without working on the book, the Chairman of the department became the lead author and fortunately he allowed me second billing. It was magnanimous of him to even allow my name to grace the cover of the book. The experience gained and my sense of accomplishment was worth all the hard work.

The responsibility for arranging for the textbook's publication was mine. A close friend owned a large printing company and agreed to print the book for cost. Additionally, he would guide me in selecting the proper paper and fonts and help design the book's jacket. Persuading the dental school's head librarian to underwrite the cost of printing was my next challenge. Since each entering class had two hundred students, one thousand copies would provide ample textbooks for five years. The Department Chairman promised to use the texts for this time period, thus assuring the sale of all printed copies. The librarian agreed to this arrangement and the price of the textbook for students was to be determined mutually by both the librarian and the Chairman. This cost was exceedingly low because of the authors' pro bono contribution and the low printing expense. Still, the sale of the books produced a small royalty which was returned to the department's Faculty Fund. If there was a penny to be found, the Faculty would know and confiscate it.

When the preliminary work on the text was finished, I anxiously awaited the return of the galley proofs from the printer.

It was the first time the entire textbook, in printing vernacular called the "blues," could be proofread for final corrections. This was the final step before going to press. I was excited!

The galley proofs arrived at my office in the early afternoon. It was an extremely busy day at my office and I did not have time to open the package. Hoping to make the 6:14 p.m. train home, I completed the dentistry for my last patient, changed into street clothes, ran out the door, made a dash for the train, and arrived with seconds to spare. Shortly, the train left the station. Though tempted to open the package containing the proofs, I decided to wait until my arrival home.

The train ride from Pennsylvania Station to the Farmingdale Station usually took one hour. At the midpoint of the journey, it began to rain. Logically, it proved that carrying an umbrella does not prevent rain. But I could smirk at those who did not have one.

By the time the train reached Farmingdale, the gentle rain had become a torrential downpour. My car was parked 200 yards from the station. The rain fell continuously, so I decided not to wait until it ended but to proceed to my car and head home. Before leaving the train, I put the galley proofs under my jacket to protect them from the inclement weather. Opening the umbrella, I descended the steps of the train and began trotting toward my car. The wind was gusting fiercely and after taking a few steps, the umbrella blew open, making it useless. I was totally unprotected from the storm. I quickened my pace and when I arrived at my car I was thoroughly soaked.

I quickly removed the galley proofs from beneath my jacket. Thank goodness the outer wrapping was only slightly damp. It appeared the proofs were not damaged by the rain. Now, there was another decision to make. It was raining so hard that the front end of the car could barely be discerned. Should I wait for the rain to stop or drive home slowly? No traffic appeared on the street and I had little fear of the storm. Rather than wait, which would have been the cautious thing to do, I started home. It was raining harder and the wind was howling.

I put the windshield wipers on high speed and turned on the defogger. I left Joe's garage where I always parked my car. Moving about ten miles per hour, I faced the storm's ferocity. With visibility almost zero, I continued driving. The slow speed was sufficient time to avoid any potential problem. Visibility improved slightly because of the white center line that reflected the car's headlights. There were no cars on the road. I decided to drive on top of the white line as a guide. If another car came along, we could always play the game called "chicken." If the white line should unexpectedly veer sharply to the left or right, I might drive onto someone's driveway. The torrential downpour was the worst I ever experienced. The wind was another factor that made driving hazardous. On occasion, lightening streaks illuminated the road improving visibility slightly. For a split second, I considered driving faster to get out of the storm sooner. However, caution dictated that safety lay in driving slowly.

The drive was tedious and filled with tension. After traveling for some time, I still did not see any other cars on the roadway. I was the only "idiot" on the road. The intelligent drivers had pulled their cars to the roadside and waited for the storm to abate. No one ever accused me of being smart. The torrential storm obliterated the street lights. Everything was pitch black. Nothing was visible except the reassuring white center line. Abruptly, the white line vanished.

The drive continued up a hill. But now there was no guideline. Descending the other side of this hill, I arrived at a point where a right turn would direct the car into a sump. Going straight would ascend another hill. The run to my home required making a left turn and driving up another steep incline. These three hills resulted in a deep valley, approximately one-half mile from my house.

There was no way to judge the amount of rain that fell and no reason to assume the sump would be full causing the water to accumulate in the valley. With a little trepidation, and maintaining my slow speed, I made a left turn onto my street. Whoosh . . . ! It felt as though the car had drifted into a deep puddle. Suddenly, the car's engine went dead. Abruptly, the windshield wipers stopped and the lights went out. My first thought was the battery had shorted out. I had no time to focus on causes. I turned the ignition off.

After a short time, I turned the ignition key. Dead! Several turns of the ignition key proved fruitless. Now my feet began to feel wet. Water was cascading into the car through the undercarriage. With the windshield wipers gone, visibility was impossible. When I rolled down my side window half way, the water level was at the top of the window's edge. I rolled the window up. I discovered the water now was above my calves. I was horrified! If I did not act quickly, I might be trapped in the car and drown. I lowered the glove compartment door, placed my right foot against it and using it for support, tried to push the car door open. The door did not budge. The outside pressure of the water was too great to open the door. There was a strong possibility of drowning.

A newspaper headline flashed through my brain; "Dentist Drowns in Car During Rainstorm." It sounded far fetched and unbelievable but it might become a reality. The water was now above my waist and continued to rise rapidly. I thought about exiting through the car's side window. But could I squeeze through? There was no other option. The water was now up to my chest. If I did not escape soon, my wife would be cashing in on my life insurance policy. For the first time, I was frightened.

The water would flood the car the moment the window was rolled down. I braced myself. Wait a minute! I am not leaving this car without the galley proofs. They were still on the passenger's seat totally under water. I would not abandon the proofs. Where were my brains, wasting time on galley proofs? Absurd! Nevertheless, I grabbed the proofs in my right hand and grasped the window handle with my left. I took a very deep breath then lowered the window. The water poured into the car. When the window was fully lowered, the car had filled with water. I put my head through the window opening and used my legs to push against the seat. I wiggled my way through the window. Completely submerged, I swam to the surface, never letting go of the galley proofs.

I swam until the water was shallow enough for me to stand. I waded out of the water. It was still raining heavily and the sky was black. The rain water was running down the road like a river. It was obvious the deluge had filled the sump, and having nowhere else to go, the water kept rising in the vortex caused by the confluent hills. My car was invisible, completely submerged under water. It had drowned! Better the car than me.

Totally exhausted and drenched, I slowly walked the half mile up the road to my home. I still protected the galley proofs by placing them under my jacket. Perhaps a futile effort, but I had to try.

When I arrived home, everyone wanted to know why I was completely soaked. Nobody believed my story until they realized my car was not in the garage. But they were still dubious. The next day, when we walked down the hill to the car and they found the ashtrays filled with water, my story became reality. It finally sank in, no pun intended, that I might have drowned if not for a little swimming skill and a lot of luck.

As expected, the galley proofs were totally destroyed. New copies arrived the following week. These proofs were delivered directly to my home to avoid any further misfortunes.

LIFE'S TRAGEDY IS THAT WE GET OLD TOO SOON AND WISE TOO LATE.

BENJAMIN FRANKLIN

TWENTY SEVEN

Testing

Cheating on examinations is a dilemma faced by many professional schools. It undermines the core mission of these institutions, which is to graduate outstanding professionals and ensure they possess the highest moral and ethical standards. A high standard of ethics should be a fundamental quality of all health professionals. Cheating taints the perpetrator and undermines the integrity of the profession. It sows the seeds for future deception and duplicity. The cheater may manipulate the results of experiments, treatment plans or take short cuts in the health care of patients that may lead to dire consequences.

At the dental school where I held professorial rank, cheating was never tolerated. Students who cheated were aware that the punishment could be severe. However, in my dental school, if you did the crime you did not necessarily do the appropriate time. The punishment for dishonesty might include a warning, a reduced grade, an extra project, or course failure. If the cheating is egregious, for example, stealing an examination, the punishment is expulsion from school. This was extremely rare.

In the 1990's, a large number of Russian students were accepted to the dental school. Many of these students were dentists in their homeland. Depending upon their prior training, an additional two to three years of schooling was required to satisfy state regulations to practice dentistry. Another group of Russian-born students was accepted to the dental school on a regular admission basis. For these students, four years of schooling was required to obtain a license to practice dentistry in this country.

As the student body swelled with Russian students, the faculty suspected an increase in cheating. On occasion, an unwarranted murmur permeated the examination room or there was irregular student movement. Some proctors noticed these disturbances but were reluctant to accuse a student of cheating based simply on body movements such as moving lips, wandering eyes, or straining necks. Other proctors refused to accuse students of cheating for fear of developing a bad reputation with the student body and be labeled a "bad guy."

In order to maintain high ethical and moral standards, many changes were made in the test taking in an attempt to reduce or eliminate cheating. Alternate seat spacing, alternate row seating, rearranging the examination booklets so one student's first page corresponded to the adjacent student's last page were some of the new protocols. Though these changes appeared to reduce cheating, the faculty was still concerned; they did not feel that cheating was completely eliminated. The pattern of murmuring and student movement persisted, suggesting cheating continued, perhaps at a reduced level. But, teachers were still reluctant to label students as cheaters.

My departmental chairman asked me to review the examination protocol, with the objective of eliminating all cheating. I accepted the assignment on the condition that I was to have complete control.

Sometimes, students are tempted to be dishonest. Due to

the intense competition, some students cheat to graduate or to attain higher grades. Elevated grades may help them secure a hospital internship or acceptance into a graduate program. My private conversations with several Russian students helped me understand the problem. In Russia, cheating is an integral part of life. Russian students come to this country and many continue this egregious behavior, as though it is an acceptable practice here.

To reduce or eliminate the problem, I decided to adopt a technique used in the military where everyone is made acutely aware of the rules of conduct and the consequences of a breach. In the military, regulations are often not enforced until they are frequently broken. When this happens, there is often a severe crackdown to emphasize that rules must be obeyed. Punishment is frequently severe and serves as an object lesson to the offender and to others. Following these crackdowns, the regulations are seldom broken. However, over time, these rules are again ignored and another crackdown often becomes necessary.

I believed cheating could be eliminated if a severe crackdown was instituted. It would be very harsh on those naive students who believed there would not be any enforcement of the rules. I felt the elimination of cheating would be achieved because my proposed sanctions would have draconian consequences. To lay the foundation for the program, a strong statement was issued to all students stating the consequences for violating the rules.

The following was presented to the students before the start of the examination:

"My name is Dr. Jones, and I have been requested by the departmental chairman to supervise the examinations in this course to ensure there will be no cheating. Therefore, the following rules are now established.

1. Anyone suspected of, or caught cheating will be asked to leave the room. This action will result in a zero as your grade on this examination. Since there are only three examinations in this course, a zero will result in an automatic failing final grade. You may be wondering why this differs from the previous rule? The answer is it does not, except that from now on this rule will be strictly enforced. The departmental chairman asked me to supervise proctoring because he knows I am an expert in detecting dishonesty. This expertise was acquired by many years of personal cheating. If there is a way to cheat, I have used it, refined it, and elevated it to the highest level of effectiveness. It appears I have been very successful considering my position and stature in the dental community. I cheated my way through Dental School, College, High School, public school, and yes, I even cheated my way through kindergarten. The fact that I have never been caught is proof of my expertise. I always understood there would be serious consequences if caught. Most important, please understand I can easily recognize and detect every form of cheating.

Now you must make a decision. Do you want to cheat and challenge my expertise, my ability to detect dishonesty? Do you want to take that chance? Is it that important to you? Understand, if I catch you cheating or suspect chicanery, you will be asked to leave the examination room. Perhaps you aren't cheating, but if I think you are you will be dismissed with a zero as your grade. If a cop gives you a ticket for speeding and you plead 'not guilty' before the judge, whom do you think the judge will believe? Similarly, if you appeal to the Dean, whom do you think he will believe?

So . . . be dishonest if you wish but be prepared to accept the consequences if you are caught. Pay attention to all instructions, for if you do not you may be suspected of cheating. Do not ask your classmate for a pencil, for an eraser, or anything, for you will be presumed to be cheating. If you have a question, raise your hand and a proctor will respond.

Shortly, I will announce the start of the examination, so please put all papers and books well out of the way to avoid any suspicion. The moment I announce the examination's start, there will be total silence even though the exam booklets have not yet been passed out. If you speak after the start of the examination, for any reason, you will be asked to leave. Are there any questions so far?

When the examination booklets are passed out, they will be placed face down on your desk. You are not to turn this booklet over until permission is given. This is done so everyone can start at the same time. I will repeat this two more times so no one will say they did not hear me or did not understand what I said. Do not turn your booklet over until I tell you to. If you turn the booklet over prematurely, you will be asked to leave the room and I will give you a zero. So . . . for the third time, sit back, relax, and when you receive your booklet do not touch it until I say it is O.K. to do so."

In the beginning, there were students who turned their booklets over too soon. They were asked to leave the room. This may appear harsh, but eventually fewer and fewer students committed this rule infraction. Were they cheating? Probably not, but they broke the rules. Now the students understood that the instructions would be strictly enforced. Word spread throughout the school that the "old" policy would be enforced with dire consequences. This was very important; it gave legitimacy to both the rules and their enforcement. The incidences of students being dismissed from the examination because of rule infractions were eventually eliminated. Lessons are quickly learned when rules are strictly enforced and punishment instituted.

By the third examination, proctors reported that they did not find any cheating. Predicated on these results, the chairman asked me to be chief proctor in other courses. Based on these new examination procedures, there was positive feedback from the student body. Generally, a handful of dishonest students change the curve and it results in unfair grades for the honest students. This reflects adversely on the overall student body. With cheating eliminated and the curve no longer undermined, the more intelligent students and those who studied harder achieved their appropriate class ranking.

For a couple of years, there were no further incidences. However, one day I noticed a female student cheating. This surprised me, since female students were seldom identified as dishonest. Her body movements were consistent with cheating. Her eyes strayed widely and her neck strained from side to side while attempting to get a better view of the adjacent student's exam booklet. Occasionally, she would look up and stare directly at me to see if her actions had been noticed. While proctoring, I look out of the corner of my eye when I suspect someone of dishonesty. In this manner, my face is turned in a different direction and the student has difficulty determining if I am watching. I was absolutely convinced she was cheating. After a short period, I pointed to her and requested her examination booklet. This is a very embarrassing moment because her classmates know exactly what it implies.

"Who, me?" she asked, as she pointed to herself.

"Yes, you," I responded. "Please hand me your booklet and kindly leave the room."

"What did I do? I didn't do anything," she frighteningly responded. I noticed a slight Russian accent but this had no bearing on the situation.

"Please pass me your examination booklet," I once again requested, this time in a commanding tone. "You know what you were doing and you are causing a disturbance and disrupting your classmates. After the exam, if you would like, I will meet you in my office where we can discuss your actions. Now, please hand me your exam booklet."

The student waddled through the row, stepping over seated students along the way. She delivered the examination booklet and left the room. After the examination, when all the booklets were collected, I exited the room and found the student waiting for me in the hallway. "What did I do? I didn't do anything," she repeated pleadingly. She was very upset and there was fear in her voice. "Let's not have this discussion in the hallway. Let's go to my office where we will have privacy," I declared.

At my office, I asked her to sit and said, "There is no question in my mind that you were cheating. You were looking at your classmates' papers on either side of you. You know it, so do I. My only choice was to request that you turn in your examination booklet. You understand this means you will fail the course. You will have a chance to retake the course and redeem yourself. I hope you have learned a lesson."

"But I did not cheat," she responded vigorously, **"I WAS ONLY TRYING TO CHEAT."**

The immediacy and originality of her defense caught me off guard. For a moment, I contemplated giving her a grade of "A" for her rather brilliant response. But then I thought, . . . isn't attempted robbery a crime?

The student received a final failing grade, retook the course, and passed. Today, she is a practicing dentist.

EVERYBODY WANTS TO GO TO HEAVEN, BUT NOBODY WANTS TO DIE.

ANONYMOUS

DYSLEXIC HAIKU

**YOU CAN LEAD A HORSE
TO DRINK HIS FILL BUT NOTHING
CAN MAKE HIM WATER.**

THE AUTHOR

Twenty Eight

Tikittu and daddy tu

My dental school graduation was wonderful and exciting. Despite several distractions, four years of extremely hard work had come to an end. One distraction during dental school was my marriage at Winter break of my freshman year. I was engaged to my future wife for three years and it was time to get married. Our honeymoon was very productive; I spent hours studying and reviewing anatomy. Another distraction was the birth of a child, a direct result of the anatomical expertise acquired during my honeymoon. This blessing was my first son, born on the first day of dental school orientation, a day designed to instill the first feelings of professionalism in students. Now there's a bunch of firsts. On this day, students learn how to obtain patients, equipment, supplies, and how to generally traverse the dental school curriculum. Because of my son's birth, I did not attend orientation. Orientation was presumed to be the beginning of my dental career for, thereafter, I would work on live patients. Despite the excitement, my son and my wife were my first priority. It took almost four months to obtain all the patient care information presented at orientation from my classmates. They were always too busy to respond to my queries.

Another diversion was a lack of money. My wife worked to generate family income prior to the birth of our child. School was my full time job. We resided with my wife's parents and though we paid no rent, we always contributed money to my in-laws for expenses. They, too, had little money and it was inappropriate not to share in the upkeep of their apartment. After the birth of our child, my wife's first responsibility was to care for the baby so she no longer worked full time. To help provide us with some income, she typed mailing labels in the apartment while the baby napped. It required the completion of many labels to earn decent money, therefore, her working hours were long and tedious. During the Christmas holidays, my wife worked as a store salesperson. I helped augment our income by working as a temporary mail clerk for the post office. During summer vacation I worked in the "soda pop" industry as a driver's helper. Though we both worked hard whenever we could, my wife and I were never able to generate enough income to pay all our meager expenses and still have money to give to my in-laws. I blessed them every day for their understanding and support.

Despite these hardships and distractions, I managed to graduate in the top 10 percent of my class and was designated a Founders Day Scholar. Additionally, I received the C.V. Mosby Award and was elected into Omicron Kappa Upsilon, the dental honor society. Most important, I was asked to teach at the dental college when my two-year tour in the United States Army Dental Corps was completed.

The decision to spend two years in the Army was necessary, a choice made by me and my wife predicated on several reasons. We were in considerable debt, had a child, and had few resources necessary to open a private dental practice. Procuring a job working for another dentist was, at best, a long shot because dentistry at that time was a cottage industry. Dentists worked for themselves and by themselves, infrequently hiring other dentists. Today, this has changed dramatically. Many dentists work for other dentists for part or all of their careers. Additionally, a military draft was in effect. By serving two years in the Army, I could avoid being called into the service after starting my own practice. This actually happened to two classmates who opened offices immediately after graduation, were called to active military duty, and subsequently had to close their practices. Finally, two years in the U.S. Army Dental Corps would allow me time to reflect upon my dental goals and objectives and further afford me the opportunity to repay some of my debt. Perhaps I could even save some money.

There were other concerns. The results of the dental licensing examination, taken in June after graduation, would not be available until mid August. What if I failed this examination? How could my family survive without sufficient income? I could get a job outside dentistry, but that would be demeaning. By accepting a direct commission in the Army Dental Corps, I would immediately earn a reasonable livelihood as an officer, become an instant gentleman, and would have the opportunity to retake the licensing examination, if I failed.

There was a two and one-half month hiatus between graduation and my Army induction. Fortunately, my wife's uncle was the manager of the Mission Orange Bottling Company in Queens, New York and he gave me a job as a driver's helper. The soda industry often hired temporary help to service the increased demand for soft drinks during the summer months and holidays. My wife's uncle was able to place me in the union on a temporary basis. Because of the union, the pay was good and my uncle frequently sent me on long trips which involved overtime pay. He knew we needed the money and my wife was one of his favorite nieces. He was a life saver. I became a dentist without a license to practice, working as a driver's helper in the soft drink industry. Was it demeaning? Absolutely not! The monetary reward was excellent, all my co-workers called me Doc, and most important, I was treated with respect. Co-workers sought my advice about their family's dental problems. I was a consultant without a portfolio, a dentist sans drill, and I loved every minute.

My job consisted mainly of delivering cases of soda to store owners. Bright and early, the driver and I would load our truck predicated on orders received the previous day, then drive our route delivering full cases, and picking up the empty cases of soda. Frequently, the delivery had to be made into a cellar beneath the store. This meant going down the cellar steps with full cases of soda and then climbing up with the empties. A full case of soda weighed approximately 35 pounds. Today, plastic has replaced the glass bottles and wooden case, cutting the weight by more than half. Sometimes the store owner provided a wooden slide. The driver would unload the truck and slide the full cases of soda down to me in the basement. These cases had to be stacked, often six high.

Climbing the stairs was the most difficult part of the job because you not only lifted your own body weight but also the weight of the case of soda. There was no conveyor belt. If you did not carry two cases at a time, it meant going up and down the stairs more times. The drivers, who were usually bigger and stronger than me, often carried three cases at a time.

Going up and down the basement steps while making store deliveries was hard work. Long trips were tantamount to a vacation. To minimize overtime during the day of delivery, the truck was loaded the day before. On delivery day, we would arrive at the plant early, punch in, get in the loaded truck, and leave. Shortly after departing from the plant, we stopped for breakfast. Usually, these trips were to some distant part of Connecticut or the New Jersey shore. The drive to Connecticut took two and one-half hours or more one way. A New Jersey shore delivery took longer. After arriving at the destination, we unloaded the truck. This took approximately two and one-half hours. We then loaded the truck with the empty cases, approximately one hour, and then drove back to Queens. Including lunch, which was one hour (union rules), the total trip often took ten to eleven hours, or more. The overtime pay was useful.

With the money earned, I began to pay off debts. I had to leave for Fort Sam Houston, Texas, August 15 for basic training. At the end of July, a letter was received from the Army with final instructions. I had to pay for my transportation to the training site in Texas, pay for my officers' uniforms, and for any other necessary expenses. On September 1, my first paycheck would cover salary for the last two weeks in August and would include reimbursement for transportation and uniform expenses. Having expended most of the earnings from my summer job, there was little money left to buy an airline ticket to Texas and buy uniforms. It was necessary to borrow money from my father-in-law to serve in the Army. What a downer.

After six weeks of basic training, I was ordered to report to Fort Leonard Wood, Missouri. Duty was requested at two other bases but the Army rarely gives you what you ask for. It appears the Army gives you the opposite of what is requested. There's the right way, the wrong way, and the Army way. The bachelor officer quarters (BOQ) became my domicile until I could find suitable accommodations for my family. It proved very difficult being away from them. There were no family quarters available, and I was placed on the post's housing waiting list.

There was no way of knowing how long the post housing wait would be and not wanting to be separated from my family, I found a rental house in Rolla, Missouri, a thirty minute drive from the base on the then famous Route 66. It was an old, dirty, dilapidated town famous for the Rolla School of Mines, which has since closed. The rental house mimicked the town with few exceptions. All the better rental apartments and houses were occupied by Rolla School of Mines' students. One day I went to the supermarket and saw two men sitting in separate rocking chairs and immediately realized it was a memorable place. They both wore blue jean coveralls, had straw hats, and I learned their names were Zeek and Elmer. It was like watching the sitcom, Beverly Hillbillies. Perhaps I could have located a house in the town of Waynesville, outside the Fort Leonard Wood entrance gate. However, when I learned the town's nickname was Gonorrhea Gulch, I did not think it was a suitable place to raise my child. The numerous strip joints were another convincing argument.

Fort Leonard Wood was a basic training post for engineers. During World War II it served as a detention camp for German prisoners of war. There were no barbed wire fences around the Fort because if a prisoner escaped there was no place to go. That is how isolated the area was.

When my wife and son arrived in Rolla in the beginning of October, she was quite disappointed. The rental house and the neighborhood made her extremely upset. Unfortunately, we were stuck with these accommodations until post housing became available. Furthermore, my wife had to remain in the house most of the time because we only had one car and I needed it to go back and forth to the base. Taking the baby for a stroll in the carriage was her only outlet because the distance to walk to shopping and stores was too great. On the weekends we went wherever she wished. This was small consolation. A furnished house was rented because, other than the baby's crib and a desk and chair, we had no furniture of our own.

We put up with this angst and lived in this house for three months. After the beginning of the new year, we were notified that on-post housing was available. We were assigned a two-bedroom house. We did not worry about furniture because the Army had a wonderful rental policy. For six dollars a month, we rented all the furniture needed, including a refrigerator, washing machine, and dryer. My wife hung curtains on the windows, we bought inexpensive throw rugs, the house looked charming, and we felt like we were in heaven.

In the beginning of our Army tour of duty we encountered a major problem: money management. The army paid everyone once a month. It took me several months to establish a workable budget so funds could be appropriately allocated to last the entire month. During basic training and while living in the BOQ, I was able to save a small amount of money. But, after paying the deposit and first month's rent for the house plus the cost of transporting my wife and son to Rolla, our savings were depleted. There was no reserve.

One month, with more than one week left until the next paycheck, we only had ten dollars in our checking account, no cash, and a bottle of milk and some baby formula remaining in the refrigerator. My wife was off the wall with fear and apprehension.

One evening, she declared angrily, "I'm going to play bingo!"

I reminded her that bingo cost ten dollars, and we only had ten dollars. That money was earmarked to last until the next paycheck.

"I don't care," she shot back forcibly. "I'm going to play bingo and I intend to win the one hundred-dollar jack pot." She said this as though she could control the numbers that would be called.

"But if you don't win," I explained, "we will have no money left and we do not get paid for another week."

"I don't care," she screamed, and with a huff hurried out the door, slamming it behind her.

She left me to watch the baby and wonder where next week's food money was to come from. I never expected her to win. To me it was an impractical decision. A few hours later my wife returned, threw a pile of cash in my face, marched into our bedroom and began crying, releasing her tension and anxiety. She had won the one hundred-dollar jackpot, so she said. For a moment, I wondered whether she worked a "trick" for the money? On many occasions my wife had remarked that the particular organ of the female anatomy most used in working a "trick" cannot be worn out. In either case, we would survive until the next paycheck. Someone was watching over us.

After moving into the house on post, life was wonderful. It was our first home. There was a play yard for our son and I put up a picket fence. Khaki is the color of choice in the Army but my wife did not think this color appropriate for a fence. I was able to barter special dentistry for white paint from a supply Sargent, extremely difficult to do, and my wife got her white picket fence. Our child could now play outside without us worrying about him walking away. In the springtime, my wife gave birth to our second child, a girl. We were prepared. The house was completely furnished, the play yard was set, and we were in paradise.

Life was wonderful. I worked in the clinic five days a week, from 7:30 a.m. to 4:30 p.m., and I was on the golf course one half hour later. I had weekends off except for infrequent duty, our finances were now regulated, and it was amazing.

Life on post was not all play. The commander established that each dentist produce a minimum number of dental procedures. It was not particularly difficult to meet these requirements. Every eight weeks we had to do hard work. In each cycle, a new batch of engineer trainees required a complete dental examination. The post's dentists had to do all these examinations in two days. Thousands of recruits had to be examined. To facilitate the examinations, a dental assistant was helpful. The soldier would sit in the dental chair, the dentist would call out his findings, and the assistant would mark them on a chart. A couple of minutes were allotted for each examination. Many of the soldiers had never been to a dentist or sat in a dental chair. One soldier sat on the foot support part of the chair and put his head where a person's bottom ordinarily would go. Several precious minutes were wasted laughing while we demonstrated the proper way of sitting in a dental chair. This happened several times, but after the first incident, nothing more was said. The dentist just bent over a little lower and continued with the examination.

There were, however, more serious times.

"Watchy'all doin' here? Y'all looks so clean in ya' white coats. Why don'tcha' git down in the mud with us real soldiers sometime?" We were back in the main clinic and that is what I heard as a soldier sat in the chair next to mine. The dentist at the adjacent chair, Captain Stephen Wolseley from South Carolina, had an angry, dismayed look on his face. He walked over to me and said,

"Didge y'all hea' what that obnoxious piece of dirt jus' said?" Steve was fuming. "Y'all can't expect betta' from them there white Southern trash. I'm gonna' fix his butt." With that he returned to his chair. The soldier was seated and draped and I heard Steve say, "How kin I help y'all, son?"

"Look man! I got this here black tooth in the fron' a my face and I wants it fixed. My Sargent tol' me to git to the dentist and they'd fix it. So here I is, so fix it."

I had never heard such disrespect. This kid was obnoxious and should be reprimanded, I thought. I fully expected Captain Wolseley to lose his cool and turn the soldier in with a reprimand.

Steve looked at the tooth and said to the patient, "I'm sorry, kid, but this hea' tooth has to be extracted, removed."

"Watchy'all mean?" the kid shot back."I wants y'all to fix it."

"Sorry, but there's no way I can fix your tooth. It's too far gone. It's got to come out."

"How the heck does you do that?" asked the soldier.

"It's a piece of cake. Don't worry, I'll take good care of y'all," responded Steve.

Steve walked over to me and told me to watch carefully. He returned to his station, took a cotton roll, and dipped it into Mercurochrome; the cotton roll was now bright red. Taking a four inch long piece of dental floss, he stuffed one end into the red-colored cotton roll, turned to the soldier and said, "Ready?"

"Ain'tcha gonna' make it numb or somethin'?" the soldier asked.

"That won't be necessary," replied Steve. "Just bite down on this," and he placed the red cotton roll between the soldier's upper and lower front teeth. The soldier thought he knew what was being placed into his mouth and his eyes bugged wide open.

"Y'all stand back," shouted Steve, "I'm doin' an extraction hea'." With that announcement he pulled out a Zippo lighter from his pocket, lit it, and placed it close to the dental floss hanging from the soldier's mouth. The soldier tightly grasped the arms of the dental chair, turned white, and began to tremble. The entire clinic was in an uproar. Steve removed the cotton roll from the kid's mouth and said, "Now git outa here and make another damn appointment. And nex' time don't be so damn obnoxious and disrespectful."

The soldier jumped out of the chair. As he walked down the aisle, he demonstrated a very suspicious gate. There is no doubt in my mind he soiled his pants.

Because of funny instances like this, but mostly because of the interesting dentistry, I looked forward to going to work every day. The clinic was close enough for me to walk to, or I could ride with a fellow officer so my wife had the use of our car and could go where she wanted. There were many activities on post for wives and my wife always participated. There were lectures on many subjects, shopping trips to St. Louis, teas, opportunity to volunteer for important projects, and of course, there was bingo.

Near the end of my two years of duty, I was asked if I would like to stay in the Army and make it a career. I thought long and hard about it. For me, the Army was wonderful. There was enough money to live well, have a home, and attain great respect. I was not only a professional but an officer. Remaining in the Army would have soon meant a promotion to the rank of Major. The military even offered to pay for specialty training.

But it was not my decision to make. After conferring with my wife, it became obvious that it was unacceptable to her.

She envisioned little stability, because we would have to move every few years. Additionally, over the course of my career I probably would have to take assignments to remote posts where my family could not follow me.

When my tour of duty was up, I went into private practice and teaching. We rented a small apartment in Brooklyn and my wife worked wonders making it into an extremely attractive home.

One day, when my daughter was about five or six years old she asked me where she was born. I told her Fort Leonard Wood. With a rising pitch in her voice she responded, "Fort Leonard Wood?" "That's correct," I replied. "As a matter of fact, you were born during an Indian attack." Lost on a young child, this response struck me as one of great levity. "Are you kidding Daddy?" she said with dismay in her voice. "What do you mean, during an Indian attack?"

"Well, you wouldn't remember because you were so young, but Indians were attacking the fort. They used bows and arrows and in fact one of the arrows came very close and almost killed you."

"Momie, Momie," she screamed as she ran to my wife, "Was I born in Fort Leonard Wood during an Indian attack?" Fortunately, my wife caught my wink and answered in the affirmative. For a few years my daughter actually believed this story and once, much to my surprise and mortification, used it in school as a "Show and Tell" presentation, complete with a bow and arrows.

My daughter eventually grew up and went to dental school. She received several awards at graduation and I was a very proud and excited father. After graduation, while standing with my daughter and many of her classmates, who also were my students, I asked her whether she recalled the story of the Indian raid on Fort Leonard Wood. She remembered, and I quickly related the story to her inquisitive friends. They got quite a kick out of the narrative.

I said to her, "Do you know what sweetheart? Based on that story, I am going to give you an Indian nickname. From now on I am going to call you "Tikittu" . . . because when you join my practice you are going to be my ticket to retirement." A roar of laughter rose from her classmates. "Gee, Dr. Jones," they all exclaimed, "that was very funny." I turned to the group which included my daughter.

"All of you are dentists now so you no longer have to refer to me as Dr. Jones. We are colleagues, so please call me by my first name, Sam." I whipped around and stared at my daughter. "But not you my dear daughter and future partner. You still have to call me Dad."

After graduation, my daughter completed training as a Prosthodontist and became my partner. I had the profound pleasure of practicing with her for thirteen years. She was truly my "Tikittu" retirement. I still consult with her.

IF YOU PICK UP A STARVING DOG AND MAKE HIM PROSPEROUS, HE WILL NOT BITE YOU; THAT IS THE PRINCIPLE DIFFERENCE BETWEEN A DOG AND A MAN.

MARK TWAIN

Twenty Nine

Liza jane

The loss of a spouse after fifty-four years of marriage is heartbreaking. It causes a melancholy that is extremely difficult to overcome. Days pass slowly and only sleep, when possible, offers some relief. This tragedy created a void in my life that was of great concern to my daughter. Her mother had passed away and my daughter was dealing with the loss in her own way. Her cat was a source of companionship and she believed a pet would serve the same purpose for me. It would help alleviate my emptiness and loneliness.

During our marriage, my wife and I had many pets. However, for the last twenty-two years she was seriously ill and not strong enough to care for a pet. Although she loved animals, she did not want to place the burden on me of sole caretaker.

When my daughter discussed the idea of getting a pet for me, I agreed. A canine would be helpful and afford me companionship. But, I insisted that it must not shed. We reviewed many interesting varieties and initially settled on the Soft Coat Wheaten Terrier. This breed had all the attributes I desired, namely, non-shedding, not too large, and a pleasing personality. Unfortunately, on further investigation, we learned the breed was notorious for chasing small animals or anything that moved. It was a runner and this could cause additional stress in my life. Imagine having to chase the animal in and out of my neighbor's yard. Who knows what scenes I might confront causing potential embarrassment. Additionally, there was a large warning sign on my neighbor's lawn: STAY OFF GRASS - TRESPASSERS WILL BE VIOLATED. We continued our research.

We discovered a breed known as a PON, an acronym for "Polski Owczarek Nizinny." It is further identified as a Polish Lowland Sheepdog. In 2001, it was recognized by the American Kennel Club (AKC) as a pure breed. Picture an Old English Sheepdog. The PON is smaller, as if someone had put an Old English Sheepdog into a clothes dryer, shrunk her, and out came a Polish Lowland Sheepdog. Furthermore, it has a stay-at-home personality. The breed is beautiful.

My daughter searched for a PON breeder and found one close to my home. Sometimes, when you find a breed you like the only animal available has to be flown cross country. A local breeder is usually the best source since information about the animal is readily available. If a problem develops there is quick access and frequently, longstanding friendships are developed between the breeder and purchaser.

The breeder informed us that a mature female was available. What a fortunate opportunity! A mature animal would be less of a burden since it was crate trained, house broken, and disciplined. The last puppy I had, (almost a "million" years ago), needed paper training. I vividly remember my growing pet having accidents, ruining carpets and chewing furniture. Of course, I would miss the joy of raising a puppy, but it would be a worthwhile trade off.

To be certain that my choice was correct, I went to my first AKC show to see an adult PON. This breed has two coats of fur. I wondered if the hot climate where I lived would cause a problem. I was assured she would be able to tolerate the heat. Of the numerous dogs I owned, my favorite was the Old English Sheepdog. Because it reminded me of this breed, my initial encounter with the PON brought tears to my eyes. I would have sworn it was an undersized or a dwarf Old English Sheepdog. I was sold, or to be more accurate, the breeder sold me Liza Jane, a five-year-old AKC Champion and mother of champions. The breeder felt she would be a perfect companion for me.

Merrilee, the attractive, charming, soft-spoken breeder thought Liza Jane should stay with me for a few days before the deal was finalized. This experience would determine if we would bond. After forty-eight hours together, I was certain we would enjoy each other. How Liza Jane felt was beyond my ability to understand. We had much in common: we both were short, attractive, and trained. My wife did a good job house training me.

Liza Jane did everything expected of her and more. I did my best to change my habits so our lives would be compatible. My new regular routine included walking, feeding, brushing her for at least ten minutes, and playing with her.

In the midst of my euphoria I did something stupid. This is not out of the ordinary for me. Liza Jane and I bonded for almost a week. Wherever I went in the house there she was, in front of me, behind me, along side me, and yes, even under my feet. When I went outside to garden, she would stand behind the glass front door and whine and make noises hoping to gain my attention. I wanted to take her outside with me while I worked on my plants and weeds. However, I had not yet purchased a long lead.

What appeared initially to be a masterstroke of brilliance backfired. It has been theorized that each gray hair on a person's head represents a dead synapse in the brain. Based upon this theory, the extent of my intelligence might be determined by my full head of gray hair.

I decided to tie Liza Jane's leash to a garbage can handle. What a stroke of genius! I assumed that she would lie on the ground and watch me work in the garden. That is precisely what happened. Tied to the can, she immediately stretched out on the driveway. Watching someone else work is my preference, too. We were kindred spirits. She was one smart lady.

Meanwhile, I prepared fungicide to spray on the Dianthus plants. After making the mixture, I started walking toward the plants. Suddenly, I heard a low, rumbling noise and I quickly turned. I could not believe my eyes. Liza Jane had gotten up and was following me. While moving forward, she dragged the entire garbage can behind her. That was the low rumbling noise I heard. Then the can began to topple. This large, green garbage can was beginning to fall on Liza Jane. For a split second, she stood motionless watching it. I could read her mind. "What the hell is going on? What the hell is that big, green 'thing' falling on me?"

She immediately pulled away from the large falling object. But this caused an unintended consequence. The rumble became louder as the can moved along the driveway and then the can hit the ground. It was empty, and this resulted in a booming sound, as though a large firecracker had gone off. Liza Jane took off, still attached to the garbage can. The rumbling became louder and she ran faster and faster. Her eyes, filled with bewilderment and fear, sought an escape route. Again, I read her mind. "What the heck is that big 'thing' chasing me? How come I'm running faster and faster and the 'thing' is running just as fast? In fact, that big 'thing' might be gaining on me." Liza Jane kept staring back at the "thing" as she ran round the driveway.

It was one of the funniest events I had ever witnessed. My

frivolity reflected a naive mind. I had not contemplated the psychological effect on Liza Jane. After a short time, exhausted, she slowed down. As Liza Jane slowed, so did the "thing." Eventually, she stood motionless in front of the entrance to the house and so did the "thing." She realized "it" was still behind her. Bewildered and frightened, Liza Jane was shaking wildly. I quickly untied her from the garbage can. Sensing freedom, she immediately darted for safety inside the house. Still traumatized, Liza Jane ran into the closed door which exacerbated her fear. I opened the door and she scooted for her crate. She retreated into the deepest portion and did not come out the rest of the day. After supper, we normally go for a walk; however, when I approached she bolted for her crate. Several days passed and our relationship did not return to normal. Now, when I take out the garbage she gives the "big green can" a wide berth. Things seem to be improving. I can only hope in her heart she will forgive me. But will she forget?

A few days later, while working in my garden, I was bitten by ants resentful of my attempt to destroy their mound. Their bites were very painful and I was certain my arm would react to their assault. I immediately took an antihistamine and searched for alcohol to swab the bites to control itching and possible infection. Not finding any, I flooded my arm with Vodka which I felt would be a suitable substitute. I sat down to read the newspaper and Liza Jane came over and began licking my arm. It felt soothing so I allowed her to continue. Shortly, she turned around and staggered into a "down" position, remaining in a dormant state for a considerable period. I had discovered a means of making Liza Jane forget: booze.

Did I tell you the purchase price for Liza Jane was insanely expensive? Did I mention that this beautiful animal who gives me so much joy and happiness was paid for by my remarkable daughter? Did I recount that through the power of creative suggestion, I tried to interest my sons in sharing the financing of Liza Jane's maintenance? Would it be indelicate to reveal that, so far, my sons are not buying into this proposal?

EVEN IF YOU ARE ON THE RIGHT TRACK, YOU'LL GET RUN OVER IF YOU JUST SIT THERE.

WILL ROGERS

THIRTY

Foreign language

Many who have mastered the English language attempt to learn another means of oral expression. Millions of dollars are spent annually on tapes and DVD's by those seeking to acquire skills in a second language.

The following is a short course to help the reader acquire an alternate language; call it Chinese 101. The articulation is enriched by reading out loud.

ENGLISH   **CHINESE**

That's not right   Sum Ting Wong
Are you harboring a fugitive?   Hu Yu Hai Ding?

I am calling you	Kum Hia Nao
Small horse	Tai Ni Po Ni
Did you go to the beach?	Wai Yu So Tan?
I bumped into a coffee table	Ai Bang Mai Ni
I think you need a face lift	Chin Tu Fat
It's very dark in here	Wai So Dim
Great	Su Pa
I thought you were on a diet?	Wai Yu Mun Ching?
He's cleaning his automobile	Wa Shing Ka
Your body odor is offensive	Yu Stin Ki Pu
Our meeting was next week	Wai Yu Kum Nao?
Staying out of sight	Lei Ying Lo
Tow away zone	No Pah King

TRANSLITERATOR UNKNOWN

THIRTY ONE

Psychology

Commuting from my home to my dental practice in New York City was my routine every working day. The round trip was seventy miles and took three hours. I would leave before the sun rose and return after dark. The Long Island Railroad trains often broke down, so I was frequently late returning home. Occasionally, inclement weather caused the train's lateness. These delays were usually less than one hour. If I missed a scheduled train because of working late, I would call home and inform them. I usually arrived home at 7:30 p.m., but often at 8:00 p.m. because of train delay.

On one occasion when I arrived home at 10:15 p.m. and pulled my car into the garage, my wife appeared in the doorway and shouted at the top of her lungs.

"Where have you been? I was worried sick and frantic. I didn't know what to do, were you in an accident, were you dead?

Damn, where the heck have you been? Why didn't you call me?" She was trembling and ghost white.

"I was stuck on the train for almost three hours, and there was no way to get to a phone. (This was before cell phones). I'm sorry, but there was nothing I could do," I replied.

"I can't take it anymore. I got so nervous and upset. I was going crazy worrying that you were hurt or even dead. I can't take it any more." She began trembling again and sobbing.

I took my wife in my arms and held her as she wept.

"Ya' know what?" I exclaimed, trying to relieve her tensions, "the kids are grown and should be on their own. You cook and clean for them and it's about time they did it for themselves. Let's sell the house and move into the city. No more commuting for me. This will never happen again."

The moment I finished, my wife began wailing. "Are you kidding? What about my beautiful house, my gardens, my shopping, my friends? Why would I want to leave all of this and move into the city?"

"To avoid this scene happening again," I retorted.

"No! No! No!" she replied and continued whimpering.

"Tell you what," I said. "I'll get a small apartment in the city and come home on weekends. That should work." This was an attempt to apply some psychology to convince her to move. I was quite sure she would not want to stay home alone during week nights and perhaps she did have some modicum of distrust.

My wife immediately stopped crying. Her back stiffened; she stared me in the face, and put her index finger under my nose. Wagging it back and forth freely, she forcibly remarked,

"No way! No way will I trust you alone in the city five nights a week."

The next day, she called the painters and a real estate agent and the process was put in motion. The house was sold and we moved into a beautiful, duplex apartment in the city. There was a professional greenhouse on one of the balconies so she had her flowers. There was plenty of shopping, and she made new friends.

I never wanted to stay in the city alone during the week and distrust was a distinct possibility. In either case, isn't psychology wonderful?

IF YOU DON'T KNOW WHERE YOU ARE GOING YOU WILL WIND UP SOMEWHERE ELSE.

YOGI BERRA

THE MAN IS THE HEAD OF THE HOUSEHOLD BUT THE WOMAN IS THE NECK.

HEBREW PROVERB

**IN EVERY REAL MAN, A CHILD IS HIDDEN
THAT WANTS TO PLAY.**

FRIEDRICH NIETZSCHE

**TO LOVE AND BE LOVED IS TO FEEL THE
SUN FROM BOTH SIDES.**

DAVID VISCOTT

THIRTY TWO

Very short stories

My wife and I were discussing our five children. We had a difference of opinion, and after awhile our voices became elevated. My wife said to me,

"You don't know what the heck you are talking about. Why don't you shut up?"

"How can you speak to me that way? I am the father of your children."

"So I told you," was her response.

────────────────────

On another occasion, we were in a heated discussion, often called an argument, about a petty issue. As usual, I started elevating my voice (shouting). My wife quietly commented,

"Let's resolve this issue once and for all. If you would like a divorce, so be it. I don't want the house; I don't want your money. I'll sign divorce papers tomorrow or as soon as they can be prepared. There is only one proviso you have to agree to." There was a long pause, and then she continued, "You have to keep the five children."

"What the heck am I going to do with five kids?"

She just stared at me, arms akimbo, with a "that's your problem" look on her face.

Once again she was the victor.

_____

My wife always looked younger than her true chronological age. Time was most gracious to her. The disparity between her appearance and her older children's ages did not jibe. One day, a neighbor asked my wife about the age of her two oldest children relative to her professed age.

"Are you sure you are not older then you are telling me? You certainly look too young to have children of that age."

"Oh, the older children are my husband's from his first marriage," was my wife's corrective response.

I had never before been married.

_____ _____

I loved dentistry and looked forward to working my entire professional life. I found that if the patient knew what to expect and was relaxed, my job was easy, enjoyable and very rewarding. To this end, I always left time for "explaining and joking" prior to doing the necessary dentistry. Mostly, it was joking. Joking with the guys was a given, but I could not believe the number of elderly, female patients who told me dirty, raunchy jokes. G-D bless them.

After the joke period, I worked without stopping until the

procedure was completed. Many times, I professed to the patient that my dentistry is free but the jokes are very expensive.

"Is it going to hurt, doctor?" was the most frequently asked question.

"Not me," was invariably my answer.

———————— ————————

To celebrate my promotion to Assistant Professor, my wife decided to throw a party. Close family, friends and a few neighbors were invited. We had only lived in our home five years and it was not completely furnished. We used our nine hundred square foot lower level for dining purposes and the kitchen functioned as the bar. Significantly, the large living room had no furniture. Custom-built cabinets were attached to the walls, but we had not yet found an appropriate dining room table and chairs. One of our neighbors, with a superior, confident attitude, questioned my wife about the lack of furniture in this room.

"Oh," my wife replied. "We put the furniture in storage so there would be space to dance."

———————— ————————

Unfortunately my wife never had the opportunity to obtain a college education. However, she is extremely intelligent (after all, didn't she marry me?), and is arguably the most left-brained person I ever met. Later in life, when our children were grown, she became a well-recognized advocate for children with learning disabilities (LD) in the Greater New York Metropolitan Area. On her own, she studied and memorized all the pertinent LD tests and their meaning. She frequently represented children at Committee of the Handicapped school meetings.

At one particular meeting, her adversary was an angry, irritable school psychologist who had a doctoral degree. At each representation by the psychologist, my wife would respond by indicating the inaccuracies and the incorrectness of her position. She was able to cite the correct information and where it could be found. Finally, the psychologist became irate and asked my wife where her authority came from.

"I don't understand what you mean by 'authority'." my wife replied.

"In other words, what degree or degrees do YOU hold that allows YOU to countermand MY authority?" the psychologist demanded to know.

"Oh," acknowledged my wife, "I have an AAD degree."

"I have never heard of that degree. What does it stand for?"

"AAD stands for 'ALSO A Doctor'."

————————— —————————

"Did you ever hear of the word 'coruscating'?" my friend once asked me.

"Sure," I replied. "It means flashing or sparkling."

"OK, smart ass," he responded, "how do you spell it?"

"I . . . T . . ." was my response.

This comeback can also be used with "that".

————————— —————————

I recently realized that the most prevalent surname in the United States is not "Smith" or "Jones" but is "Speaking." I wondered how a name could be speaking, but that is another issue.

The number of people at the other end of the telephone line who identified themselves using "Speaking" as their last name, for example, Joe Speaking or Sally Speaking, is remarkable.

I can recall conversing with hundreds, perhaps thousands of people with that surname.

The proof of this theory lies in the frequency of the occurrence. The large number of persons with this last name inevitably leads me to conclude they are probably related, perhaps sisters, brothers, or cousins.

The theory states that "everyone 'speaking' is related." This relationship certainly brings everyone in the world closer making the world smaller. A logical extension of this theory is the corollary that the reader and the writer of this piece must be related because their fathers are fathers.

There is another large, often heard family surname, namely, "I'll be right back." One evening, a waiter approached my table and said,

"I'm Joe; I'll be right back."

I remarked that he had an extended family with many others having that long, funny last name.

As he walked away from the table, he said,

"Oh, no. That's my middle name. My last name is 'soon'."

————————— —————————

Observation After living in Florida for the past several years, I recently had the opportunity and pleasure of returning to New York for a brief visit. I immediately noticed the disparity in the number of overweight women when comparing the two locations. When walking the streets in New York City, you count the number of overweight women by the handful; in Florida you count them by the hundreds.

Perhaps this results from the faster northern pace which provides additional exercise, resulting in less body fat? Perhaps it is a gene phenomenon? Or, perhaps the hot Florida sun creates laziness and discourages women from working off excess calories? Another explanation might be deduced by examining a map of the United States. When viewed on a wall, it is obvious that the State of Florida is below New York State. Is it possible that women with excessive weight are inevitably pulled to a lower position by the force of gravity? ¿Quién sabe?

THE OLDER I GET THE BETTER I WAS.

ANONYMOUS

A TEAR SHED FOR ALL THAT HAS BEEN AND NEVER WILL BE AGAIN IS A MOMENT WELL SPENT.

DAVID SPELTS

Thirty Three

English lovers

I do not profess to know French, Spanish, or other languages. Because it is so confusing, I cannot even speak a good English, and writing in my native tongue makes me dizzy. Let's face it, English is a crazy language. Witness the following:

> We'll begin with a box and the plural is boxes,
> but the plural of ox is oxen, not oxes.
> Then one fowl is a goose, but two are called geese,
> yet the plural of moose should never be meese.
> You may find a lone mouse or a nest full of mice,
> yet the plural of house is houses, not hice.
> If the plural of man is always called men,
> why shouldn't the plural of pan be called pen?
> If I spoke of my foot and show you my feet,
> and I give you a boot, would a pair be called beet?
> If one is a tooth and a whole set are teeth,
> why shouldn't the plural of booth be called beeth?
> Then one may be that, and three would be those,
> yet hat in the plural would never be hose.

And the plural of cat is cats, not cose.
We speak of a brother and also of brethren,
but though we say mother, we never say methren.
Then the masculine pronouns are he, his, and him,
but imagine the feminine, she, shis, and shim.
So English I fancy you will agree,
Is the craziest language you ever did see.

–Author Unknown

Confused? Then ponder the following:

1. The bandage was wound around the wound.
2. The farm was used to produce produce.
3. The dump was full so it had to refuse more refuse.
4. We must polish the Polish furniture.
5. He could lead if he would get the lead out.
6. The soldier deserted his dessert in the desert.
7. Since there is no time like the present, he thought it
    was time to present the present.
8. A bass was painted on the head of the bass drum.
9. When shot at, the dove dove into the bushes.
10. I did not object to the object.
11. The insurance was invalid for the invalid.
12. The oarsmen had a row about how to row.
13. They were too close to the door to close it.
14. When does are near a buck does funny things.
15. A seamstress and a sewer fell into a sewer line.
16. The farmer taught his sow to sow seed.
17. The sailor could wind the sail in the strong wind.
18. I shed a tear upon seeing the tear in the painting.
19. I had to subject the subject to a series of tests.
20. Can I intimate this to my most intimate friend?

I will confuse you further with the succeeding examples:

There is no egg in eggplant, nor ham in hamburger; neither apple or pine in pineapple. English muffins weren't invented in England or French fries in France. Sweetmeats are candies while sweetbreads, which aren't sweet, are meat.

We take English for granted. But if we explore its paradoxes, we find that quicksand can work slowly, boxing rings are square, and a guinea pig is neither from Guinea nor is it a pig. And why is it that writers write but fingers don't fing, grocers don't groce, and hammers don't ham? Doesn't it seem crazy that you can make amends but not one amend?

If teachers taught, why don't preachers praught? If a vegetarian eats vegetables, what does a humanitarian eat? In what language do people recite at a play and play at a recital? Ship by truck and send cargo by ship? Have noses that run and feet that smell?

How can a slim chance and a fat chance be the same, while a wise man and a wise guy are opposites? You have to marvel at the unique lunacy of a language in which your house can burn up as it burns down, in which you fill in a form by filling it out and in which an alarm goes off by going on.

English was invented by people, not computers, and it reflects the creativity of the human race, which, of course, is not a race at all. That is why when the stars are out, they are visible, but when the lights are out, they are invisible.

There is a two-letter word that perhaps
has more meanings than any other
two-letter word, and that is
"UP"
Follow along carefully.

It is easy to understand UP, meaning toward the sky or at the top of the list, but when we awaken in the morning, why do we wake UP? At a meeting, why does a topic come UP? Why do we speak UP and why are the officers UP for election and why is it UP to the secretary to write UP a report?

We call UP our friends. And we use it to brighten UP a room, polish UP the silver, we warm UP the leftovers and clean UP the kitchen. We lock UP the house and some guys fix UP the old car. At other times the little word has real special meaning. People stir UP trouble, line UP for tickets, work UP an appetite, and think UP excuses. To be dressed is one thing but to be dressed UP is special.

And this UP is confusing: A drain must be opened UP because it is stopped UP. We open UP a store in the morning but we close it UP at night.

We seem to be pretty mixed UP about UP. To be knowledgeable about the proper uses of UP, look the word UP in the dictionary. In a desk-sized dictionary, it takes UP almost one-quarter of the page and can add UP to about thirty definitions. If you are UP to it, you might try building UP a list of the many ways UP is used. It will take UP a lot of your time, but if you don't give UP, you may wind UP with a hundred or more. When it threatens to rain, we say it is clouding UP. When the sun comes out we say it is clearing UP.

When it rains, it wets the earth and often messes things UP. When it doesn't rain for awhile, things dry UP.

One could go on and on, but I'll wrap it UP for now because my time is UP, so . . . it's time to shut UP!

Oh . . . one more thing. What is the first thing you do in the morning and the last thing you do at night? **U P**

The above was adapted from various comical messages published on the Internet. The sources are unknown.

The English language is constantly changing. For example, the Washington Post's Mensa Invitational asked readers to take any word from the dictionary, alter it by adding, subtracting, or changing one letter, and supply a new definition. The following are the 2005 winners.

1. Cashtration (n): The act of buying a house, which renders the subject financially impotent for an indefinite period.
2. Intaxication: Euphoria at getting a tax refund, which lasts until you realize it was your money to start with.
3. Reintarnation: Coming back to life as a hillbilly.
4. Bozone (n): The substance surrounding stupid people that stops bright ideas from penetrating. The bozone layer, unfortunately, shows little sign of breaking down in the near future.
5. Foreploy: Any misrepresentation about yourself for the purpose of getting laid.
6. Giraffiti: Vandalism spray-painted very high.
7. Sarchasm: The gulf between the author of sarcastic wit and the person who doesn't get it.
8. Inoculatte: To take coffee intravenously when you are running late.
9. Hipatitis: Terminal coolness.
10. Osteopornosis: A degenerate disease. (This one got extra credit)
11. Karmageddon: It's like, when everybody is like, sending off all these really bad vibes, right? And then, like, the Earth explodes and it's, like, a serious summer.
12. Decafalon (n): The grueling event of getting through the day consuming only things that are good for you.
13. Glibido: All talk and no action.
14. Doepler effect: The tendency of stupid ideas to seem smarter when they come at you rapidly.
15. Arachnoleptic fit (n): The frantic dance you perform

just after you've accidently walked through a spider web.

16. Beelzbug (n): Satan in the form of a mosquito, that gets into your bedroom at three in the morning and cannot be cast out.

17. Caterpallor (n): The color you turn after finding half a worm in the fruit you're eating.

The pick of the literature was:

18. Ignoranus: A person who's both stupid and an asshole.

Perhaps, in the future, these 'new' words will show UP in standard, accepted dictionaries.

The Washington Post has also published the winning submissions to its yearly contest, in which readers are asked to supply alternate meanings for common words.

And the winners are:

1. Coffee, n. The person upon whom one coughs.

2. Flabbergasted, adj. Appalled by discovering how much weight one has gained.

3. Abdicate, v. To give up all hope of ever having a flat stomach.

4. Esplanade, v. To attempt an explanation while drunk.

5. Willy-nilly, adj. Impotent.

6. Negligent, adj. Absentmindedly answering the door when wearing only a nightgown.

7. Lymph, v. To walk with a lisp.

8. Gargoyle, n. Olive-flavored mouthwash.

9. Flatulence, n. Emergency vehicle that picks up someone who has been run over by a steamroller.

10. Balderdash, n. A rapidly receding hairline.

11. Testicle, n. A humorous question on an exam.
12. Rectitude, n. The formal, dignified bearing adopted by proctologists.
13. Pokemon, n. A Rastaferian proctologist.
14. Oyster, n. A person who sprinkles his conversation with Yiddishisms.
15. Circumvent, n. An opening in the front of boxer shorts worn by Jewish men.

POLITICAL LANGUAGE PERVERSION:

Research has led to the discovery of the heaviest element yet known to science. The new element, Governmentium (Gv), has one neutron, 25 assistant neutrons, 88 deputy neutrons, and 198 assistant deputy neutrons, giving it an atomic mass of 312.

These 312 particles are held together by forces called morons, which are surrounded by vast quantities of lepton-like particles called peons. Since Governmentium has no electrons, it is inert; however, it can be detected because it impedes every reaction with which it comes into contact. A minute amount of Governmentium can cause a reaction, normally taking less than a second, to take from four days to four years to complete.

Governmentium has a normal half-life of 2-6 years; it does not decay, but instead undergoes a reorganization in which a portion of the assistant neutrons and deputy neutrons exchange places. In fact, Governmentium's mass will actually increase over time, since each reorganization will cause morons to fuse with neutrons, forming isodopes.

This characteristic of morons leads some scientists to believe that Governmentium is formed whenever morons reach a critical concentration. This hypothetical quantity is referred to as a critical morass.

When catalyzed by money, Governmentium becomes Admnistratium, an element that radiates as much energy as Governmentium since it has half as many peons but twice as many morons.

Anonymous Political Activist

I am reminded of the story about four people named Everybody, Somebody, Anybody, and Nobody. There was an important job to be done and Everybody was sure Somebody would do it. Anybody could have done it, but Nobody did it. Somebody got angry with that because it was Everybody's job. Everybody thought Anybody could do it, but Nobody realized that Everybody wouldn't do it. It ended up Everybody blamed Somebody when Nobody did what Anybody could have done.

From a source long lost from memory.

**Not to be redundant,
but the English language is crazy.**

WORDS ARE, OF COURSE, THE MOST POWERFUL DRUG USED BY MANKIND.

RUDYARD KIPLING

IF YOU DON'T HAVE TIME TO DO IT RIGHT YOU MUST HAVE TIME TO DO IT AGAIN.

ANONYMOUS

THIRY FOUR

Good night sweet princess

My life began when I met my future wife. At that time, Bella was a mature, erudite sixteen year old and I was not quite eighteen. She was the only girlfriend ever in my life. From the beginning, she tried to keep me humble and grounded and helped shape the person I am today. Already in college, I was young and wild. Bella was a settling influence. She impressed upon me the importance of education. Often, our dates were at the library where she read short stories while I attended to my studies. Bella was strong-willed, determined and had the insight to see our future together.

Her early life was shaped by a domineering father, a delightful, caring mother, an overpowering older sister and the stresses of having a cerebral palsied older brother. Bella was a warm, caring, supportive and understanding woman.

Bella was an extremely loyal person. She had a very close friend. They went to school together and played hooky together. As time passed, marriage and new families resulted in their being separated by distance. Yet, every day they spoke to each other by telephone. Bella once confessed to me that Cathy was more like a best sister than a close friend.

Bella had strong personal beliefs. Some individuals erroneously believed she was forceful and always wanted her way. This is a distortion of the facts. The truth is simple; my wife and I mastered the art of compromise. Our system was unique: I admitted I was wrong and she agreed. Whenever we had a disagreement we would discuss the matter continuously, intellectually and objectively until she was right. When her father became ill from depression, Bella, who was in her early twenties and the youngest child, took control of the family. She kept the family together through determination and strength until her father recovered. Even at a young age, her actions were always mature and thoughtful which made her stand apart from others. Like the North star, she was bright and constant.

Bella had just passed her nineteenth birthday when we married. I was in dental school and we could only afford a brief honeymoon. Bella worked full time to support us. She always made certain the environment was quiet when I studied. She was my rock, my guiding light. My job was to study and graduate dental school. Bella was there to help me be successful. She had admirable qualities as a wife: loving, intelligent, hard working, understanding, and supportive. Occasionally, she even helped me wash the dishes. The one thing my wife lacked was good health.

It all began in 1986. Prior to this date, other than a broken ankle and the relatively common female hysterectomy, Bella had few medical problems. She was a strong, robust woman who raised five children, four of them boys, tolerated an obstinate, strong-minded husband and was the mistress of a large home. Bella was not particularly enamored with sports, yet dutifully drove the kids to their soccer and little league baseball games. Playing baseball with her was an exasperating experience. She had a strong throwing arm but her aim was erratic. When accurate, her hard throws hurt the children's hands. When her throws went awry, the kids had to chase and retrieve the ball from long distances. They would yell, "Mom, you always ask us to be straight and direct. Why can't you throw the ball the same way?"

Bella felt that doing something worthwhile is never easy. She epitomized proaction. "If you need help," Bella would say, "I have two hands. They are small, but they're strong." It wasn't enough to talk about something, you had to fight for what is right and initiate the appropriate action to make certain it happened. In the late 1970's, Bella formed an organization called, "Parents Concerned With Academics" and was its first president. The organization became a voice for students with learning disabilities and dyslexia. She made presentations to state and local authorities and represented children at educational meetings for the handicapped. These dialogues helped prepare educators for the children's needs. Bella and her organization demanded understanding and support from the public schools for these special students. She organized a picket of the New York State Department of Education in Albany, New York to help advance the rights of these children. It was the first time this Department was ever picketed. She wasn't just an advocate for these children; she was a whole movement.

Bella had a quiet but profound sense of humor which helped her withstand the family stresses she faced constantly. Her religious convictions were a further source of great strength. She cared deeply about her faith and insisted all her children be Bar or Bat Mitzvah. Once, I suggested we not spend money on a big party but, instead, take the entire family, including grandparents, to Israel. "Absolutely not," she replied emotionally. "Celebrating our children's coming of age at thirteen is a singular event. We can go to Israel anytime."

My wife adored our children to the point of spoiling them. The word "no" was rarely used and infrequently enforced. Bella understood the word "empathy" more than anyone I've ever met. She shared the feelings of her children with insight, understanding and compassion. She did this with energy, optimism, determination and incredible cheer added in for good measure. Our daughter, Lois, received a scholarship to Boston University. After she completed her sophomore year, Bella said to her, "You know what sweetheart, your scholarship saved the family a lot of money and you deserve a reward. Your father and I would love to send you on a trip to England. But, you can't go alone. Maybe you can ask one of your friends if they can go with you?"

A few weeks passed and I asked Lois if she found someone to go with her on the trip. Smiling, she replied, "Oh, yes. I decided to choose my best friend . . . Mom!" I nearly collapsed. It had to be a conspiracy. Paying the expenses for two travelers was not what I budgeted. However, a man's two greatest assets are a closed mouth and an open wallet. It wasn't fair but they deserved the reward.

In 1986, Bella's life changed dramatically. She became plagued with a series of severe medical problems. For the next twenty-two years, Bella would withstand numerous medical assaults on her life. These "medical wars" slowly but continuously sapped her strength. People respond differently to adverse health events in their lives. Through each ordeal, Bella never stopped fighting. Each day she would look for the sun to rise. Life was too short to wait for sunset. She maintained her dignity and spirit and was steadfast in her determination to overcome each ailment. Bella, laughing or crying, can best be described by one word: valiant.

My wife's first major illness compromised her heart and required a quadruple bypass operation. After the diagnosis, she expressed relief knowing the source of her problem and that it could be corrected. She had not been feeling well for a considerable time and now knew the reason. She never had a heart attack but suffered from constant angina. She took the diagnosis seriously because her father had died of a heart attack at age sixty-one. Facing death, Bella went through countless emotions; fear, sadness, shock, confusion and anger. Bella was only fifty-two years old at the time, rather young for such a medical condition.

My wife had heart surgery six months after we moved from Long Island to New York City and exactly one week before our thirty-third wedding anniversary. Bella loved lobster. By befriending a hospital director, I was able to arrange a candlelight, catered lobster dinner with champagne on Christmas Eve to celebrate both her successful surgery and our anniversary. It was a total surprise to her and I am certain it helped speed her recovery. She gave me a big smile, a sexy wink and then remarked that she owed me a gift. My thoughts made me blush.

Before she fully recuperated, my wife developed stage II diabetes. Our physician believed that the bypass surgery was the inciting mechanism, though there was a history of diabetes in her family. Soon after the onset of the diabetes, Bella contracted acute idiopathic autoimmune hemolytic anemia. This is a disease of a sudden onset where her immune system identifies her red blood cells as dangerous foreign bodies and destroys them. This illness was life threatening. For more than two years, she received large doses of prednisone accompanied by frequent blood transfusions. Bella constantly complained of tiredness but would not give up her strenuous regimen. She had to persevere until tomorrow because, for her, looking back was not helpful. On many occasions, she promised to live to see all her children reach adulthood. Furthermore, Bella refused to die until she had grandchildren. Finally, the anemia was resolved, but not before she developed bleeding behind her eyes which threatened her eyesight.

For the next few years Bella did well. There appeared to be no repercussions from the heart surgery or the anemia. By living in the city where my dental practice was located, the prior long commute from Long Island was eliminated. This enabled us to spend more time together during her recuperation. These were exciting times. As her strength increased, we took advantage of the many interesting places in Manhattan. There were Broadway shows, movies and museums to see. Dinner out became commonplace. She was a gourmet as long as she ate one of her favorite foods: steak, potatoes, lobster or shrimp.

Bella's specialties were shopping, decorating and spending money, not necessarily in that order. She had an unlimited budget and always exceeded it. Bella had the uncanny ability to walk into a shop, notice an object, comment on its beauty and then discover it was the most expensive item in the store. She had exquisite taste and frequently bought expensive items to decorate our home. Fortunately, not always. Not knowing how long she would live and not having any grandchildren, Bella compensated by collecting dolls. They could be found throughout the apartment. These dolls became her grand kids. She selected them with care and spared no expense purchasing them.

Several of our friend's asked Bella to help decorate their homes. Her personal taste was eclectic but she always adhered to her "client's" preference. She never earned a penny for these favors. Bella enjoyed spending time decorating our new duplex apartment. She knew though plans are made, life is what happens. For the most part, she was able to forget about the medical problems that plagued her.

Bella loved growing flowers. The upper balcony of our apartment was converted into a greenhouse where she could grow daisies, lilies and assorted house plants. Completely enclosed, the temperature, moisture, and sunlight were controlled by the turn of a dial. She loved growing plants and having fresh flowers in the apartment, especially in the winter. So did I! Bella especially loved orchids, but could never get them to grow. She would spend hundreds of dollars buying these exotic plants. With orchids, her touch was their demise. It saddened her when the flower would bloom and then subsequently die. On several occasions, she remarked that it was fortunate that those who cared for her health were better doctors than she was a horticulturist. My wife was more successful with growing plants at our previous home on Long Island. Bella did not grow orchids there but we had a special arrangement for gardening. I was the designated digger; her responsibility was plant selection and location. I excavated a suitable hole and placed the plant. If the plant bloomed, she would take the credit; if the plant died, it was my fault. Bella frequently admonished me not to give up my day job.

One afternoon, after arriving home, I went directly to my bedroom to change into relaxing clothes. When I entered the room, Bella was clothed in a nightgown, sitting on our bed. This was unusual for her this early in the afternoon. She had a blank stare on her face, as though she was gazing into space. It struck me as very peculiar.

"Are you OK, honey? What seems to be the matter?" I inquired in a concerned voice.

"I don't feel good," was her slurred reply.

I again inquired and received a mumbled, incoherent response. I touched her head and she felt feverish.

"All right, let's get dressed and run over to the Cornell Hospital Emergency room." Our physician warned us that Bella's anemia problem might return or her heart could act up again. If this happened, we were to go to the hospital immediately. Suddenly, she became unresponsive making it impossible for me to dress her. I needed help so I called 911.

Bella was laying on the bed unconscious when the paramedics arrived. They immediately put her on an IV drip. Her breathing was extremely shallow and her blood pressure dangerously low. They transported her to Cornell Hospital. I followed and went directly to the emergency room. When I arrived, Bella was still connected to the IV with the addition of an antibiotic.

The attending physician believed my wife had an infection. He explained that it was imperative to identify the specific organism so the appropriate antibiotic could be administered. The antibiotic initially given to her was considered a stopgap measure. Her temperature was 103° and had risen since her admission to the emergency room: a bad sign. At about 6:00 p.m., her temperature rose to 104.5°. The laboratory tests did not identify the specific organism causing the infection.

The prognosis was very serious. I telephoned my daughter who lived three blocks from the hospital. After I explained the situation to her, there was a profound silence at the other end. Finally, my daughter said, "I'll be there immediately." By the time my daughter arrived, Bella's condition had further deteriorated. She was moved to a permanent room at about 11:00 p.m. Her temperature continued to rise and at two a.m. she was taken to intensive care. Her condition was very grave.

The final diagnosis revealed that Bella had developed a rare kidney abscess of unknown origin. The attending surgeons wanted to operate, but due to her frailty our cardiologist believed it was inadvisable. He felt she would not survive the procedure. The nephrologist prescribed massive doses of cipro, an antibiotic, and miraculously the abscess disappeared. Later, we learned that few patients afflicted with this type of abscess survive. It is a testament to my wife's stamina and her feisty will to live. She had once promised to outlive me just to ensure my woeful existence. I believe she stayed alive to fulfill this promise.

Bella was comatose for three weeks. This resulted in a severe reduction of muscle mass which left her extremely weak. After recovering from the coma, she did not have sufficient strength to use a fork to eat nor could she stand unsupported. For her remaining years, Bella was relegated to ambulatory assistance equipment: a cane, a walker, a wheelchair or a scooter.

My wife spent three weeks in a rehabilitation hospital. Upon returning home, she faced a major dilemma. Bella was able to move around using a walker; however, the duplex apartment had stairs. It was impossible for her to make the climb. She could use the hall elevator, but from our door it was a considerable distance down the hallway. There was insufficient space in the apartment to maneuver a scooter, so Bella was relegated to using a wheelchair. Her arms were weak, so she frequently lost control and banged into the walls, especially when she had to pass through a doorway. Entering the elevator presented another problem. The doors would begin to close before she could get in or out. Her elevator journeys evoked animal-like noises and screams, loud enough to wake up the dead. Her raucous outbursts were occasionally accompanied by unladylike swear words. However, her commitment to overcome her physical problem was exceptional. Bella used the wheelchair every day until she was strong enough to walk up and down the stairs. It was a time that tested her spirit. Bella was undaunted and resolute. She would say to me, "I am going to get better if it kills me."

In 2000, we discovered Bella had breast cancer. It was another challenge, but she was unshakable. Her mother died of breast cancer. Her indomitable will would not allow that to happen to her. She would surmount this new obstacle. I had just retired and now was able to devote 100 percent of my time to her. Bella suffered through a lumpectomy, followed by chemotherapy and radiation therapy. This resulted in baldness, constant nausea, vomiting, and increased weakness. In spite of all this adversity, Bella was glad that she only needed a lumpectomy. She was able to retain her full figure and did not need a prosthesis with its concomitant plastic surgery. She often told me, "I want to be whole." After each chemotherapy treatment, we would walk until we found a restaurant. Bella would indulge in all the foods she loved; lobster, shrimp, pastrami, pickles, hot dogs and of course dessert. All desserts were welcomed. She often said, "There are no bad desserts - just some are better than others."

Bella developed a love for wigs of all colors, styles and lengths. She enjoyed shopping for expensive wigs while listening to me insist that bald women are sexy. I tried to convince her that head coverings are a short term proposition. "Don't spend too much money for them." She did not listen to any of my logical arguments. "When you look good, you feel good," she insisted. "Besides, I am worth every penny and I intend to buy the most expensive wigs available." She kept her promise.

With humor and determination, Bella persevered and won. Her philosophy was simple. "When you discover that you may have a terminal illness, you go through a period of tears and anxiety. But, once you learn to live with the diagnosis and the treatment you can benefit from humor. You have to laugh at adversity because being sad and adopting a 'why me' attitude is not helpful and only wastes time." She believed laughter was especially beneficial to those under stress. Humor was an invaluable tool for my wife. It helped her stay calm and reduced the stresses on her health. After completing her treatments, she was declared free of breast cancer. It remained so for the rest of her life.

After the conclusion of her cancer therapy in 2001, we relocated to our retirement home in Florida. Shortly after our move, Bella began having trouble with her back. She was diagnosed with osteoporosis, an age related softening of the bones. The disease caused the vertebrae of her spine to weaken and collapse resulting in painful fractures. Every vertebra in her spine was affected. After learning that she needed back surgery, my wife stoically remarked, "Here we go again!"

Bella had great strength but even the most valiant people occasionally succumb to feelings of self pity and despair. Soon she became morose and despondent. "Why is this happening to me? What have I done to deserve all of these problems?" Our lives were complicated and interrupted by trips to Shands Hospital and overnight stays in motels. My wife became increasingly depressed. Her pain was excruciating. Heavy doses of narcotics were prescribed to alleviate her discomfort, but Bella did not react well to the morphine derivatives and frequently went into a hallucinatory state. On one occasion, I was watching television when she walked out of the bedroom pushing her walker. She was stark naked! For Bella, a rather reserved person, this was not normal. Startled, I asked, "Do you know you have no clothes on?" She looked herself over carefully, stared back at me and curtly responded, "So!" The narcotic had rocketed her into outer space.

All the surgical procedures proved unsuccessful. Bella was relegated to back pain for the remainder of her life. On a scale of one to ten, with ten the worst possible, her pain constantly registered a five or six, frequently climbing to nine or ten. Non-narcotic pain medication helped moderately. She endured and lived with this pain constantly, another testament to her courageous spirit.

The next few years were good to us. We went on a cruise and made several short trips. Every week, we went to our club for karaoke night. We listened to musical noises while we ate and drank. Though Bella knew she could not sing, she could discriminate between good and bad singing. However, she was complimentary to all no matter how poorly they sang. Bella always ended the evening with dessert.

One day, we decided to take a trip to Disney World. Still terribly weak but mobile, she relied heavily on a cane or walker and sometimes a wheelchair. To avoid pushing Bella around all day in a wheelchair, I rented a battery-operated scooter. It was the first time she had driven such a vehicle. For the first few morning hours, Bella drove into everything, whether it moved or not. By the afternoon, she began to feel more confident. At one point, she pulled alongside an elderly gentleman who was sitting on his own scooter. Bella looked at the gentleman and he gazed back. With a serious look on her face, she said to the man, "Want to race?" The man looked at my wife incredulously. Bella returned a demure smile. She was ready for the Indianapolis 500 Speedway.

In 2005, events took a turn for the worse. Bella broke her hip. Five months later, she broke her other hip. The surgeons believed that due to her advanced osteoporosis, the hip breaks were classical cases of brittle bone structure. Both hips were replaced with titanium. Now my "bionic" wife (she also had steel ligatures in her chest from the bypass operation as well as titanium implants throughout her mouth) was relegated to a walker on good days, which were few, and a wheelchair or scooter on others. No more canes. At one visit to the doctor, she asked him when she could have sex? "As soon as you get rid of your husband," he replied.

Her spinal compression fractures and the two hip replacements caused Bella major problems dressing, especially when she had to bend. She felt insecure bathing or showering without assistance. Additionally, she could no longer clean the house, not that she ever relished the job. Her idea of housework was sweeping the room with a glance. She believed that everything belongs in a given place, but if something was not where it should be, it was not a big deal. Housekeeping was not one of her favorite pastimes. Now, these tasks were relegated to me. I had to put my glass in the dishwasher, remove my dirty dishes from the table and put my worn clothes in the hamper. Heavy chores such as closets, rooms, floors and toilets were left to a housekeeper. My mother did not raise a dummy.

Bella was a fantastic cook. Now, she could not stand long enough to prepare meals. This job devolved upon me. I was upset over having to cook but that was nothing compared to having to eat my own cooking. With Bella's guidance, I became a reasonable cook, at least no one got sick. However, there were many meals I destroyed. Once, after a particularly unappetizing excuse for a meal Bella commented, "As a cook, you make a great dentist." I had tried but she was correct.

A perturbing factor in our life was my inability to care for Bella twenty-four hours a day, seven days a week. Our salvation was a long term health care insurance policy purchased twelve years earlier. Among other things, it paid for health aides who provided constant companionship for Bella. This gave me time to shop for food, prepare meals, go bike riding, and do other activities to help maintain my strength so that I could take care of my wife.

My wife loved one aide in particular. Josette cared for Bella with love and devotion as though they were mother and daughter. They always seemed to be on the same page, giggling simultaneously about something funny. Occasionally, Bella would call her "Rosette" and Josette would get upset, then realize it was just one of Bella's moments. On good days, Josette would take her to lunch or go shopping with her. This made Bella feel like a whole, useful person. Josette had a full time job and could only care for my wife two or three times a week. On these days, there was always a smile on Bella's face and her disposition improved considerably. Josette's companionship surpassed any possible medication. She was the sunshine in my wife's life.

Besides keeping me in line, Bella's other purpose in life was to constantly test the acumen of the medical profession. One year later, we discovered that she had stage III lung cancer. It was a cancer of considerable size but, thankfully, had not metastasized to other parts of her body. Treatment consisted of radiation therapy five days a week for seven weeks accompanied by one chemotherapy session each week. Unfortunately, surgery was not realistic because Bella was too fragile. When this course of therapy was completed, she was given two weeks rest followed by an additional series of chemotherapy treatments for seven weeks. Considering her past medical history, she regarded this new setback as just another bump on life's highway.

Bella understood the odds of being cured were slim. However, she was determined to defy the statistics again. Her health was poor and she was weak from previous ailments. She became increasingly weaker but she never lost her confidence. Bella was determined to complete every treatment and be a winner once again. She was heroic.

While undergoing radiation and chemotherapy treatments, my wife again lost most of her hair. She still had the previously purchased wigs. However, her baldness no longer concerned her because she could not go anywhere. Bella did not have the strength to leave the house except for medical treatments. The therapies were exhausting. Additionally, we had to drive almost two hours round trip each day to the cancer center. When she was not eating or having treatments, Bella was in bed sleeping. Fortunately, these treatments caused her few problems with nausea and vomiting.

Amazingly, she still had a hearty appetite. My wife did not have to exist on foods like mashed potatoes or macaroni and cheese. Bella appeared to be on a sea food diet; she would see food and consume it. She would devour all the food on her plate and often eat some of mine. After consuming the main course, she often complained of being "full." In these instances, when asked if she wished to forgo dessert, Bella invariably remarked, "There is always room for dessert."

In addition to the responsibility of doing all the cooking, I inherited the job of doing the dishes. I developed dishpan hands and cracking skin. I was worried about developing an infection and safety became an issue. However, I remembered that nothing bad can happen to a man while doing the dishes. At one point, I contemplated going back to work to support her eating habit. Preparing meals occupied most of my time. Repetition had improved my cooking abilities and Bella complained less frequently. After a particularly good meal, there was a spicy moment when I asked Bella what her favorite dish was. "You," she replied. The single constant throughout the prolonged course of Bella's treatments was her prodigious appetite and passion for food.

After completing the radiation and chemotherapy programs, a PET scan revealed the cancerous lesion had shrunk 50 percent and was dormant. Her cancer was in remission. The oncologist commented, "This is beyond my wildest dream." His plan was to closely monitor the situation and take another PET scan in three months.

This subsequent PET scan report revealed, "a slight increase in activity in the lung which may be due to inflammation, although a residual/recurrent tumor cannot be ruled out." This news was unnerving. Was it simply an inflammation or a disastrous reactivity of the cancer? The pulmonologist who had made the original diagnosis suggested that another bronchoscopy be performed. This approach involves looking directly into the lungs whereby the physician can determine whether it is an inflammation or recurrent cancer.

After completing the procedure, the pulmonologist noted that a well-defined lesion was evident at the original bronchoscopy. He then said, "After careful scrutiny, there is evidence of inflammation, but no lesion is visible." He continued, "To make sure, cells were collected from a broad area of the lung and sent to the laboratory to test for cancer." Several days later, he telephoned and reported the biopsy revealed no evidence of cancer cells. In his opinion, Bella was cancer free.

When the pulmonologist called, Bella was napping. I immediately walked into the bedroom and gently shook her. "Honey," I happily announced, "I have wonderful news. You no longer have cancer." Bella slowly opened her eyes and stared at me quizzically. Did she hear me? She was not wearing her hearing aids, so I said, a little louder, "Did you hear me? You no longer have cancer. The doctor just called and said the biopsy was negative. You are cancer free."

Her eyes opened wider, and a broad, know-it-all smile illuminated her face. Bella knew she would win and beat the odds again. With an innocent, girlish gaze she stared at me for a few seconds, and then asked,

"What's for supper?"

She had returned to what had sustained her through all her illnesses: food.

Bella was sick for many years. She was always in pain yet through her many illnesses she retained a positive spirit. When she was lucid, times were wonderful. When she was not lucid, or when she was forgetful, I lived on fond memories forever part of my life.

During these strenuous times, our grandchildren were very small and a blessing for my wife. Bella had only seen them a couple of times. She loved them but, unfortunately, did not know them. Another blessing was our children. They were aware of their mother's deteriorating health and were in constant contact, always offering support. Bella was a wonderful mother and deserved their accolades and attention.

The children were concerned about the consequences in the event our money ran out or if I got sick and was unable to supervise their mother's care. Each child offered to take Mom into their home and care for her. It was a sincere and heartwarming offer but not very practical. They had their own lives and I did not feel they would be able to undertake and handle such a difficult situation. Knowing my children, they would find a way to care for her. I promised myself never to let that happen. Bella was free of lung cancer. She still had good days and bad days but the agonizing uncertainty of whether she had cancer was gone.

One day, after having ambulatory surgery, I returned home in the afternoon extremely tired, in pain, uncomfortable, and woozy from the anesthesia. Bella, recognizing my discomfort, called to me from across the room.

"Sweetheart," she exclaimed. "Could you please come over here?"

I waddled across the room. Taking small, painful, duck-like steps, I approached her and replied, "Sure. What do you need?"

With a big, broad smile she looked deep into my eyes and said, "I love you."

I smiled recalling all our wonderful yesterdays and the possibility of a better tomorrow. After more than fifty-five years together and through all her tribulations we were still one. She was feeling my pain and discomfort. I asked her if I could give her a big kiss?

"Sure," she replied.

"Would you like a kiss on the lips or on your cheek?"

"The lips would be better," she replied.

Bella died on May 18, 2008. Now, I only hear the silence. Good night sweet princess. The world was a better place with you.

Thirty Five

Last will and testament

Fortunately my wife and I were able to accumulate a considerable amount of wealth during our lifetime. This prosperity was derived from my dental practice, lucky real estate investments, and advice from a most competent, talented, and an honest investment counselor. Raised in a lower middle income environment, our parents always taught us the value of money. They provided nourishing food for the table, a roof over our heads, but very few amenities. Family cash flow was very poor, bills consuming most of their income. As an example, my father paid for my college and dental school tuition by borrowing from the value of his whole life insurance policy. When he passed, I paid all of his outstanding obligations. Payback is a "bitch."

After a short period working in my profession, my wife and I were providing our children with many comforts, sleep away camp and travel to a foreign country among them. As time passed, we mused over our accumulated wealth. Though my children are successful in their own vocations, should they received a large amount of cash upon our death they might use it frivolously. We believe the harder one works to accumulate riches, the more it is appreciated. Additionally, we feel that if we do not go first class then our children will.

Accordingly, we decided to add an addendum to our last will and testament. This codicil reads as follows:

> *Dear children:*
> *When mother and I depart this earth, please bury us with dispatch. Being of sound mind and body, we declare that we have tried to use all our assets before our demise. If there is any money left, it is our mistake.*

LIFE'S TOUGH . . . IT'S EVEN TOUGHER IF YOU'RE STUPID.

JOHN WAYNE

LaVergne, TN USA
05 January 2011
211298LV00002B/3/P